Signet

Ellia Ember

Table of Contents

1

Odette

ROAR!

I ran around my room, arms all tiny like the arms on that creature our kingdom archaeologist dug up last year. I was a dinosaur, and my fancy dresses were my prey.

Most people would say this kind of behavior was "unbecoming" of a princess, and I should be wearing dresses and having tea parties and practicing for when I grew up and became queen.

I didn't care. This was much more fun.

A knock on the door pulled me out of my dinosaur fantasy.

I turned back into myself as I pulled the door open and beamed up at my father.

"That was quite a roar I heard," he said. "What are you pretending to be today? Are you still the wolf people from the woods, or something new?"

I put my hands behind my back, swaying back and forth proudly. "Something new. Wolf people got boring after a while. Also, I realized I was never going to be able to scratch my ear with my toes. I can make my arms all tiny though. Look."

Father chuckled. He was always so pleased with my games. He was the reason I knew the word "unbecoming," and it was because he said, "I don't care what you think is unbecoming of a Princess, King Roderick, my Odette will play however she likes."

Then he pretended to be a giant bird with me in front of King Roderick from Oldsword, and we never saw him again.

"We'll find a new backup prince for if Prince James refuses to meet her," said my father to my mother on a way out of the ugly castle the ugly king made even uglier by being there.

I didn't know what that meant, but I *did* know who Prince James was.

He was the prince of the kingdom with a castle just across the way, on the other side of the forest. Our border was actually somewhere in the middle of the forest, but it was so "treacherous" according to mother that nobody ever crossed the forest to get over to his kingdom.

You had to take the long route across the river, around the edge of our lands into his. I always wanted to visit him, because I loved the idea of sailing on a big ship, but I hadn't gotten to so far.

Oh well. I was only seven. There was always time, and maybe this summer would be it. My tutor was away for the next three months, so I could do whatever I liked all day.

My personal plan was to play dinosaurs and maybe make some friends who didn't abandon me for their other friends like my *old* friends did. It would be a first.

"Come here and sit down a minute, will you, Odette?" said father, pulling me out of my sailboat, dinosaur, and friendship fantasies.

"Yes, father?" I bounced on the bed, and he bounced me back so I giggled. I didn't do it again though, because he had his serious face on. This must've had something to do with royal duties.

"This summer we're going to do things a little differently," said father.

"We're not going to our summer house?"

Father shook his head. "No. Do you remember us telling you about the Prince from the town on the other side of the forest? The one who gave you that?"

Father pointed at the white heart cushion on my bed. I went to sleep cuddling it every night. The prince from the nearest kingdom gave it to me when I was a baby, and I'd never let it go.

"Prince James," I said, nodding, with confidence.

"Well, this summer you're going to meet him for the first time since you were a baby. We're going to spend the entire summer with Prince James and his mother, Queen Eugenia Bertha. How does that sound?"

My jaw dropped. "You mean I get to go on a boat? And make friends? And *go on a boat?*"

Father chuckled. "Yes, Odette. You get to go on a boat."

With a shriek, I leaped up and wrapped my arms around his neck. "Perfect. That sounds perfect. That's exactly what I wanted to do this summer." I pulled back a second. "Wait. Why are we going?"

Father had an expression I couldn't make any sense of. After thinking for a moment, he said, "Because your mother and I, and Queen Eugenia Bertha, would like you and Prince James to become friends. Would you like that?"

I shrieked again and gave my father another hug. "Oh, yes please. I know I've always wanted to have more friends. Those girls I used to be friends with were *so* rude, so I've always wondered what it's like to be friends with a boy. There are so few boys around this kingdom. Just girls. I mean, there's that boy, Jaunty, who comes here with mother's beauty team sometimes, but I don't understand what he says half the time. But he's very funny even though I don't know what he's saying."

Was I rambling? The girls I used to be friends with said I did that a lot. They didn't seem to like it, and from the weary look on father's face, I worried he might feel the same.

"Yes, jaunty is quite a character, alright," said father, and the weariness left him. "But I can promise you, you *will* understand what Prince James is saying. He's a very mature and well-spoken little boy. I met him just a few weeks ago, when I was arranging this trip. I'm sure you two will be the best of friends."

Friend. A *friend* sounded nice, but maybe not a best one.

I already had a *best* friend, who I ran out to tell the good news to immediately, but I probably needed another best friend considering how my current best friend hopped around the little pond in our garden when I tried to enthuse about how I was going to go make new friends with a boy.

Frogs couldn't talk, so maybe our friendship was completely one-sided anyway.

"Is he talking back yet?" asked mother.

I jumped almost as high as the frog. Her barefoot approach was always so silent. Most other peoples' shoes made big clunking noises on the stepping stones that wove a path along the grass leading to this little secluded corner of the garden.

She seemed to be having one of her more carefree days. Her long golden hair, so much nicer and easier to tame than mine, hung loose by her shoulders, only gently tussled by the wind. She wore one of her plain dresses. Those were the kind of dresses I liked, when I was forced into wearing one at all.

"Not yet," I grinned. "But maybe someday."

Mother guffawed. "The day an animal talks back to you is the day I stop breathing."

I folded my arms defiantly. "Well, I'll just have to find a talking animal and make sure you *don't* stop breathing so I can prove you wrong."

"Well, you just might do that. If anyone can find a talking animal, it will be you."

Mother approached tentatively, but instead of crouching in the dirt with me, she sat delicately on the bench like a proper lady. There was a part of me that wanted to be just like her, but most of me wanted to stay just like I was because it was much more fun.

"I hear your father told you about the new friend you'll be making this summer."

If there was anything that could get me to bound out of the dirt and hop onto the wooden bench—hurting myself in the process—it was that.

"Yes! I can't wait. Friends. And friends with a *boy*. That's so cool and grown-up."

"Yes, and he's around two years older than you, so you'll feel even more grown-up. Well, he *will* be this summer, anyway. You'll get to celebrate his birthday with him, and he yours."

Two years older than me? Since I'd be 8 in August ... Wow. He was turning 10. That was double digits! I was dreaming about the that day almost as much as was dreaming about my Coming-of-Age, or perhaps my coming into adulthood.

I'd be 20 when I came of age, and 18 I reached adulthood. They seemed like a lifetime away. Heck, my coming of age was almost *two whole* lifetimes away for me!

That was math my tutor would be proud of.

"I'll do my best to be super mature and impress him," I declared.

"You do that," said mother. She put her arm around me and pulled me into her side the way I always loved her to do. "No, actually, you just be yourself, Odette. I'm sure he'll love you for it."

I scratched my face. "Love me? No, that's gross. I don't want boys to love me. I just want to be friends with them."

"What, not even when you grow up?"

I shook my head defiantly. "I want to be like Aunt May, all grown-up and all alone with lots of friends but no husband or anything. It seems much better."

Mother sighed, but she still smiled. "I'm afraid that's not possible for you, Odette. One day, you will be Queen, and you need a King by your side so you can produce an heir. Well, I suppose you could also have a Queen by your side, and you two could adopt an air. But it would be easier if it was King."

I folded my arms. "I want neither."

Mother sighed again. "You might change your mind when you're older. You haven't fallen in love yet, and that can change your perception significantly. And I really hope you do change your mind. Because this kingdom, and Prince James's kingdom, need a set of monarchs without the messy past of who's currently ruling. They haven't had a normal monarchy in years. You remember how I told you that your father was never supposed to be King."

I nodded. "Uncle Frederick died young. So even though father gave him the throne—"

"Abdicated by means of refusal to take power," said mother.

"Yes, that. Even though father did that, he had to take the throne back."

"Yes, then have you." She tapped my nose slightly. "Our little miracle. Because I was nearing the age I wouldn't be able to safely have little you any more."

I folded my arms. I knew mother had more lines on her face and more loose skin around her neck then other mothers of children my age, but she was talking like she was old. She was definitely not old.

She was only nearing 50. There were people who lived to 100. How could she be old when there were people alive who were twice her age!?

"So because it was messy when father took the throne, I have to make it not messy when I do?" I asked, folding my arms.

"Yes. And so does Prince James, which is why I think you two will make a wonderful match. Queen Eugenia Bertha and King Gregory were never supposed to take the throne, either. And she most certainly didn't think she'd end up as queen all by herself so soon afterwards."

I frowned. "What happened to King Gregory?"

"I don't know. He took unexpectedly ill, and that was it. Such a tragic event, but at least it wasn't as grisly as what happened to his brother."

"What happened to his brother?"

Mother winced. "Let's just say, there's a reason we don't let you go near the woods or talk to the people who can turn into animals inside it. But you're far too young for the actual story."

My arms were already folded, but I unfolded them and re–folded them for emphasis. She knew well I was annoyed by how I wasn't allowed to talk to those people. They could turn into animals! How cool was that? It was my dream to be able to do that someday, but I knew I'd never be able to. You had to be born into that, and I was born into royalty instead.

"So because it was all messy when you and father and when James's parents took the throne, James and I need to be friends?"

"Yes, Odette, ideally. You know, we've actually been arranging this for some time. There's a reason Prince James gave you that cushion when you were very young. It was because this was always meant to be. You and Prince James were always meant to meet each other, and hopefully one day, you two will be King and Queen of *both* of our kingdoms and take on your royal duties amicably, simply, and with no fuss."

I blinked several times.

Wait.

I wasn't just going to be friends with this boy? I was supposed to *marry* him when I grew up? After I told mother I didn't want to get married?

I pouted and turned from her, now understanding that this wasn't just a happy little friendship, but a royal duty after all. The duties had always been my least favorite part of being royal.

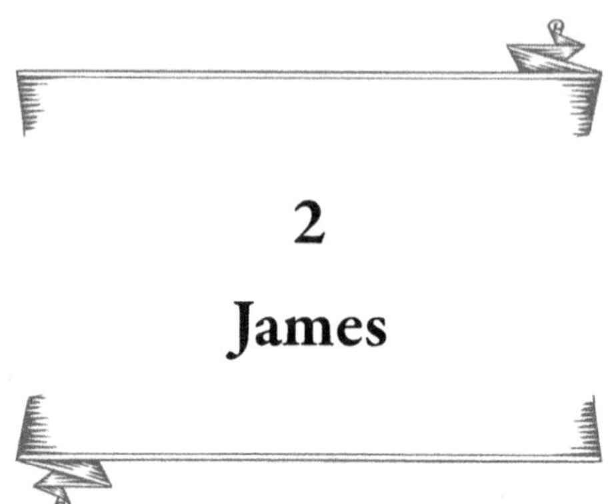

2

James

I couldn't lie, I was kind of annoyed at being made play with a 7-year-old, but I guessed it was for ... what was the word? Inter-kingdom relationship strengthening or something?

So for the good of the people and the monarchy, I'd do it. I mean, she was a princess. She wasn't like the normal 7-year-olds who ran around the castle and the surrounding town shrieking their heads off like idiots.

"Back straight, James," mother urged, "and don't be afraid. You have to go forward and take her hand, give her a proper welcome to our kingdom. There's no need to be shy."

I frowned up at her. "I'm not shy. I'm just trying to look all formal."

"Oh. Well ... well, loosen up a little bit. You can't seem like you're shy, or *she'll* be shy, and we need this to go well."

"I know. For the good of the kingdom. I heard you and Bertram talking. We need more money, so we need to be allies with them."

Mother looked mortified. I couldn't help but grin at that.

"Well, keep that to yourself, alright?" she said. "Look, here they come!"

Mother placed her hands firmly on my shoulders, her many rings weighing on me. She always wore those rings when doing official royal duties, and I thought they looked terrible. Then again, I thought these shoes and my golden chains looked terrible too, but when you were a royal, you had to look the part.

The horse-drawn carriage trundled forward, crunching along the dirt ground as it wound up through a maze of grass and hedges in front of our castle.

I tried not to let myself wince as a cloud of dirt washed towards us, thankfully falling fast. There was no wind to make the sun more tolerable, so nothing to carry the dirt and whip it at us a few more times.

The sun was still a problem, but at least it was morning. I wouldn't be baked alive in my heavy royal clothing until at least noon, and I could change before then.

There was this bubble in my stomach that I recognized as the same kind of excitement that came up when I was waiting for a present or something. I was a little pleased about making a new friend. I didn't have any royal friends.

My best friend, Don, was the son of a Lord, and the boys we sometimes played with were also sons of nobles and such. But an actual royal? The closest I had was one of my cousins, and I wasn't allowed to see him very much because he lived far away and came from "a different kind of pack."

The carriage came to a halt. The man steering it leaped down into the dirt, sending one last little cloud flying. As soon as I was king, I'd replace these dirt trails with that hard black stuff people churned in those big barrels with fires under them. Tar? Yeah, that. I'd replace all the roads with it if I could. It would be better for our town, and by extension, our entire kingdom, and I only wanted the best for us.

The man open the door to the carriage, and out stepped King Richard of Swansdale. I hadn't seen him since I was two. He was very old, but still so regal. His thick hair and beard were well groomed and streaked heavily with grey.

He wore a long, elegant cloak hemmed with fur I was sure he was melting in, and it covered a finely draped suit as he turned towards us and approached.

"Queen Eugenia Bertha," said King Richard, bowing low. "And little Prince James. Not so little anymore. What a strapping young man you've become."

I rolled back my shoulders and puffed out my chest.

"Please, Richard, call me Euberta. And where is Odette?"

King Richard turned back towards the carriage, where a scuffing noise was coming from. I automatically frowned but fixed my face immediately, fearing mother's command to do so. I didn't want to be corrected in public. I needed to be perfect. The perfect Prince to perform his princely ... duties. Was there a word beginning with "P" for "duties"?

The fizzy feeling in my stomach intensified as the scuffing turned into distinct footsteps. I expected a perfect little princess to step out, like something you saw in a young girl's dollhouse, with a nice frilly dress and perfect hair to curtsy and play perfect royals with me.

Instead, my mouth fell open as a little girl with wild curls, dirt on her nose, and a pair of overalls peeped out and approached.

"Odette!" cried King Richard. "Where are your shoes?"

"I didn't want to put them back on. It's too hot for them, father!"

There was a hiss over my shoulder, right into my ear.

"Fix your face!"

I winced, but at least mother had whispered.

"Mother ... are you sure that's a princess?"

"Certain," said mother. "I know, I *know* she's probably not what you expected. But princesses in her kingdom don't have to dress regally until they're 13 years old, and even then, they only have to do so when making official appearances. She's still a princess, James, and I promise, she's lovely by what her parents tell me."

Queen Lithe stepped out behind her daughter, holding a pair of scruffy shoes. The princess approached and grabbed the edges of a phantom dress to curtsy. Alright, she was scruffy, but at least she was kind of funny.

"Pleased to meet you, Prince James. And I'm honored to meet you, Queen Eugenia Bertha."

"Oh, call me Queen Euberta," said mother.

I actually had to talk now. My voice came out all stuttery and pathetic. "Pleased to meet you, Princess Odette," I said.

Oh no. Now I actually *was* shy. Her ragged appearance threw me, so it took me a minute and a prod from mother to reach out, take her hand, and kiss it with a wince.

It felt weird. It felt wrong. It felt like I was greeting some random child in the street.

She gave me a look up and down, and I was sure she didn't like what she saw, either. Of course she didn't. Why would a little girl who didn't want to dress in royal clothes like a little boy who did?

"And it's an honor to meet you, King Richard and Queen Lithe," I said, feeling like I was just rattling off lines I'd learned for a play.

Odette's mother chuckled. "How sweet. Very charming. I'm sure you and our Odette will get along splendidly."

I looked up and down again, from her dirty feet to her untamed hair, and I wasn't so sure. But then I remembered mother was always telling me that appearance didn't make a person, who they were inside did, so I figured I should give it a shot at least.

"Would you like to see my shooting range?" I asked Odette.

Her eyes sparkled. "Oh, yes please."

Maybe this wouldn't be so bad, after all.

"Mother? Can we go?"

"Of course, dear." Mother stepped closer to me, leaned down, and whispered, "and you can change now if you like."

"No. I think I'll stay like this. Someone should show her how a royal should dress."

And before mother could say anything against me, I gestured for Odette to follow and set off towards the front doors of the castle, well ahead of our parents.

"Thank you for having me," said Odette. She was a few paces to my right. "I ... I, um, I've never visited another royal castle before. I've never even been in another kingdom. Our summer house is in another town, but it's still in our kingdom. I've never been on a boat before either. That was fun. Have you ever been on a boat?"

She winced, and I wasn't surprised. She'd said something really weird. A royal who'd never been on a boat? That was, like ... as I said, really weird.

"Lots of times. Why have *you* never been on a boat?"

Odette shrugged. I waited for her to speak, but it didn't seem like she was going to. It was very unbecoming of a royal to simply shrug without speaking.

Once in the castle, we took a shortcut out one of the side doors, skirted down the side of the castle, and headed for the back. Odette gave our treehouse a good look on the way. Was that somewhere I needed to invite her to see? I didn't have to, right? It was mine and Don's. Our secret place. Odette and I could find somewhere else to be our spot.

Like, if she wanted to, obviously.

After crossing a couple of gardens in silence, we passed through an arch and stopped at a dirt-covered yard covered in targets. The weaponry, a little stone building with a rickety door, stood to the left. I dipped in to grab my favorite bow and slither of arrows, which I equipped.

"This is where I go to do my princely duties of slaying opposing knights and soldiers who want to threaten our kingdom," I said brightly.

Odette's face crumpled.

"Do you actually slay opposing knights and soldiers?"

"No, but I might have to one day. To protect our kingdom."

Odette rolled her eyes. "I don't think killing is very nice."

"No, but sometimes you have to do it to protect yourself."

"Father says there are other ways. Imprisonment, forced labor, and that kind of thing."

"Well, none of those things actually work, you know." She raised her eyebrows at me, and I didn't want an argument so I just scoffed. "Look, it's not like our kingdom gets attacked very often anyway. This isn't 200 years ago or anything. We're all peaceful now, so let's just drop it."

Odette nodded. "Okay. Well, it's a very nice training area. I like all the different targets at different heights. We have something like that, too."

"Really?" Maybe she was a little interesting after all. Maybe this attire made sense. She didn't want to get nice clothes dirty! "Do you like training, then?"

Odette shrugged. "I've tried it, but it gets very boring after a while. I just learned enough to protect myself in emergencies. I can hit the middle of most targets. I don't think I'm going to be doing any more, though. I much prefer helping take care of the horses and doing their shoes and things."

"But that's not a royal job. That's a servant's job."

"No, it's the job of whoever chooses to do it. And I choose to do it. It's fun. It mean, not the cleaning the horses out part, but the rest of it. Have you ever seen how horseshoes are made? There are these long sticks and they go in the fire, and the horseshoes go all red and—"

"I don't like blacksmithing," I said curtly. "It's very dirty. I only visit blacksmiths when I'm going on monthly royal rounds with mother to check in on all the local businesses and see how well they're doing."

Odette folded her arms. "What, is all you do royal duty stuff?"

"No!" I folded my arms. "I'm still a child. I play sometimes too, you know."

"Yeah? What do you play?"

There was a laugh behind us, and I turned around to see Bertram, mother's right-hand man, had approached. He chuckled so hard that it tussled his perfect grey hair which was usually so rigid it never moved.

"Oh, James, please. You act like your playing isn't just an extension of your royal duties, too." He rolled his eyes and looked down at Odette. "He plays

Kings and Nobles with his friend Don. And hello, by the way. The Queen sent me to introduce myself. My name is Bertram, and should you ever need anything night or day, I'm the one you can come to. And if you tell tales on little Prince James to me, I'll make sure they get back to his mother."

Bertram gave a wink.

"Pleased to meet you, Mr. Bertram," said Odette. "I love your accent. It sounds like the accents that are described in books set on the landmass across the big ocean. Actually, that's what the Queen sounds like, too."

"Yes, yes, that landmass is where were both from," said Bertram, his eyes lighting up far more than they ever did when I spoke to him. "I met the Queen when I was just a boy. We became unlikely friends. She insisted I travel over here with her when her parents moved here when she was just a teenager. We didn't seem like we be friends at first, because we were from such different worlds, but things have a way of working themselves out. Don't they, Prince James?"

He raised an eyebrow at me. I had a feeling he was here to keep an eye and make sure I was playing nice.

"Yes, they do," I muttered.

"Alright. Now, I'll be waiting for you in the entrance hall to show you to your room when you're done out here with the Prince," said Bertram, "so take your time, as I've been tasked with nothing but looking out for you today, Princess. I'll be ready when you are. It was a pleasure to meet you."

Bertram turned, gave me a commanding look, and left. Odette smiled.

"I like him," she said. She looked very sincere, but that expression was replaced by a smirk soon after. "So. Kings and Nobles? What does that entail?"

Maybe that smirk was just what she looked like when she smiled. Or like, *one* of the ways she looked when she smiled. She didn't *have* to be teasing me.

Maybe she be interested in this. She looked like the type to play, and she was younger than me, so she'd definitely be into pretend games.

I gestured for her to follow me into the nearest garden, just beyond the training grounds. There was a little statue of a throne in there that I hopped up into.

"I sit here, and I order Don around to practice for when I'm King. It's very good fun. He plays the Lord, he plays my servant, he plays a peasant, he plays a chef ... oh, and one time he played my Queen. That was really fun, and we pretended to get drunk at a big dinner, but a big battle happened so we had to wander around drunk trying to control everything and make everything okay again. It's all good practice, you know, because these things can actually happen."

There was a ghost of a smile on Odette's face, like she liked the idea of games, but there was something wrong. I rolled my eyes, and she rolled hers right back.

"I don't know what *you're* rolling your eyes for," said Odette. "Even your games are all ... silly. Do you *really* do anything other than being a perfect prince all the time? You're an almost-10 year old boy. All the 10-year-old boys I know of are more adventurous. They run around and get dirty and they go on hikes and adventures and stuff like that."

I folded my arms. "I don't like that. It's not very productive."

"You like productivity, then?"

"Yes. I like doing things that will benefit my kingdom and my family in the future. Why? Don't you?"

"No. I like doing things I find fun. Like pretending to be a dinosaur and attacking all the dresses I don't like, watching the blacksmith work, talking to animals, playing in the garden, oh, and reading. Oh, and we play games sometimes too. Board games and cards and stuff."

Oh, those games. We had a game room, but I hadn't been in there a long time. It was my father's. He liked to sit in there and drink beer and spend money.

Games ... I sighed.

Mother's voice popped into my head, telling me this had to go well, and I wondered if I ought to resurrect the game room and make it a place fit for Odette just so she wouldn't keep staring me like I had three heads or something.

"Well, good for you," I said. I hopped out of my throne, suddenly wishing I didn't have to entertain this girl because it was clear we weren't going to get along. "You know, I think I have a letter to write to one of my other royal contacts, so do you mind if we go inside and I go to my room? Bertram is waiting on you, anyway. You'll be taken care of and fine in there. You can ... play one of your little *dining sore* games. What *is* dining sore?"

Odette blinked at me again like I had three heads and I'd just started sprouting more.

"Dinosaur. They're these big giant creatures. The archaeologist who works in my castle found a lot of bones that created this huge skeleton of a giant lizard creature with tiny little arms and a really long tail. It has huge jaws, and he thinks it lived before humans did. Millions and millions of years ago. Big monsters. Ever since it was discovered last year, all the kids in my town run around pretending to be them and savaging each other. It's a much better game than pretending to be King, because you're going to have to do that for real anyway when you grow up. But dinosaurs don't exist anymore so you have to use your imagination."

Gosh, she could ramble, couldn't she? I kind of liked that, though, because so could I.

And I needed to ask mother about these dinosaur things, because that actually sounded really cool. I wasn't going to take Odette's word for it, because for all I knew she was making it up to try and get back at me for doing things she didn't like.

Maybe she just wanted to make her life seem so much cooler than mine, when clearly I was the one who had it all.

"Well ... okay," I muttered. "Like I said, I need to go into my room. No, my *office*. So we can go back and you can go off with Bertram."

She followed me into the castle in silence. Once she greeted Bertram, I left without a word, figuring she was well taken care of.

Once they vanished up some stairs, I left the way I came, heading back outside for my throne which was also my favorite spot to brood. When I arrived, my worries melted away when I saw who had to be the only sane person our age in the castle.

"Did the princess arrive yet?" asked Don. He dressed a lot like Odette, but he wasn't *royal*, and he was kind of goofy looking so it suited him. At least *he* wore *shoes,* though.

"Yeah. But she's not very much like a princess. She dresses weird and thinks royal duties are stupid."

"Really? So does she not have a choice in being here, then? If she thinks royal duties are stupid?"

I shrugged. "She probably doesn't. But this isn't much of a royal duty for her, anyway, is it? Our parents are the ones who need to get along. It's just easier for them if we do, too."

Don shook his head, making my frown deepen. "No, no, I heard my parents talking about how your parents and the princess's parents want you two to get along so when you grow up you'll get married. Your parents don't need to get along at all. *You and her* do."

"No!"

It couldn't be true. Mother wasn't trying to marry me off, was she? Especially not to *her*.

But Don would never lie. He never had before and had no reason to.

"My father said that your mother said you don't *have t*o marry her, but they want you to spend time together so you can make ... an informing decision when you grow up."

"Informed decision," I said. Mother said it a lot around me. "And I've already made mine. I'm *not* marrying her."

"Hear hear," said Don.

He moved out of the way so we could share my throne, and I hopped into it with my arms folded. Maybe I *would* be brooding here, after all.

3
Odette

U^{gh.}

I didn't think it was possible to dread the coming summer any more than I already did, but here I was.

I usually adored my anonymous trips into town with my parents. Today's was just with mother, and she put face paints on me so I could run freely and play with some people my age like a normal person for once.

Instead, all I got was harassment and a ball kicked at my head from some boys around James's age.

Was there a switch inside boys that made them extra obnoxious at 15? I supposed I'd have to see, but then again, James had never been particularly nice at any age.

I was upset that whole first summer, wondering why he didn't like me and what I ever did wrong. He, his friend Don, and I were forced together most days, wandering around and doing our own activities. But James had this high and mighty attitude.

We had a few nice encounters where I thought we could be friends. He opened up his game room every few days and we played cards and board games, but he was restless, and he didn't like losing.

My second summer, I tried to avoid the game room because he was so bratty in it during the first. Bertram said to ignore him.

"The prince is used to getting everything he wants," said Bertram, shrugging, "and it's high time he learned life doesn't work that way. It's a good thing you beat him so badly last summer, princess."

But my avoiding the game room just led to James getting all huffy and spending his time with Don.

"Look, if you don't like our games, then you don't have to play," said James, whenever I tried to tag along and didn't have a good time. "There's plenty to do around here. Go find something."

"But your mother says you're supposed to spend time with *me*," I insisted.

"I'm playing with Don," said James.

I couldn't say I was surprised. He wasn't the first to disobey his parents and run off with someone else when I was involved.

I took to wandering the grounds of his castle, and I made friends with the blacksmith. Outside of watching her work, I spent a lot of time with Bertram and recounted how James brushed me off for Don.

"That little prince is getting too big for his boots," said Bertram disapprovingly, and even though he reprimanded James and demanded he include me in his games, it never lasted long.

"It's not really a good game for little kids anyway," said James, which sent me off *fuming*.

"I'll give him a good talking to," Bertram stated towards the end of the summer. "You'll see. Next year, he'll be a perfect gentleman. I hope."

He wasn't.

The next summer wasn't so bad; Don was away with his family, so James had nobody to ignore me for. It didn't stop James's high and mighty attitude from leaking through as we spent many of our days wandering the edges of the nearby woods, riding horses through the grounds, and doing a little training together because I was so bored and tired of listening to him talk about nothing.

Admittedly, the training was fun. It was nice to hit targets, and it was the first time James smiled at me since the obviously false one when we first met.

But I got bored of that quickly so I left him to his own devices and wandered back to the blacksmith to watch her work. When James found me there an hour later, he rolled his eyes as he did every time he found me doing something he disapproved of. I always rolled my eyes right back. By the end of the summer, I was doing it automatically whenever he approached.

By next summer, I was rolling my eyes at the mere mention of James's name. My father disapproved of it highly and told me I had to be nice. That earned my father an eye roll, too, but I did my best to obey.

James and Don had outgrown games now. It was all jousting and fake sword fights from then on, and they never wanted to include me.

"You're too little," said James.

"Oh, come on. Give her a shot," said Don.

They did, but when I backed into a tree for more cover, some of the branches tangled in my hair and put me out of the game. I had to admit I was grateful. I didn't see the fun in waving a fake sword around.

"See, I told you we shouldn't have let her play," said James.

On days Don wasn't around, James finally paid some attention to me, begrudgingly going into the game room and losing badly often.

He won rarely, and when he did, he was worse than when he lost. When he was on a streak, he didn't want to stop, even if I fell asleep at the game table.

Towards the end of the summer, he made an effort. That was probably because I saw his mother and Bertram giving him a stern talking to once more. The day after, he showed me the library I'd only *thought* about entering. He watched me read for two hours before he fell asleep at one of the tables.

We went out on horses a few times over the following days, and even went through the town with a guard once. James had such a smug expression and a snooty little wave as people surrounded us and cheered. That removed my desire to repeat the experience.

"It was nice to see you two had a few good days," said mother, on the boat ride back home at the end of the summer. "He seems to be making an effort. Maybe next year, you can bring something you like that you can do together."

I wrote that as a note to myself, and so the next summer I brought a big pile of fossils with me, just lots of little bones that our kingdom archaeologist—now calling himself a paleontologist—let me take, but *only if I kept them really, really safe.*

As a result, James and Don spent almost the entire summer fossil hunting and digging up things in the woods. When I pointed out that I was pleased James was finally doing something for fun, he got all snippy and defensive.

He did end up apologizing, and we had a pleasant time when the three of us discovered a huge leg bone together and sent for my castle's paleontologist at once, and for the next several days we were praised highly throughout the castle as it turned out we discovered the bone of a yet-undiscovered species of dinosaur.

When I pointed out that it was James who chose the place to dig after I got some high praise, he mentioned that it was me that brought the little fossils that got him interested in the first place, and I gave him my first genuine smile.

We dug and dug for the rest of the summer, but we found nothing as exciting as the leg. There were a few pottery fragments that turned out to be 2,000 years old, though.

But towards the end of the summer James grew more insufferable as he boasted of his new talent for finding old things. That, paired with the bratty teenage boys I'd just met in town, made the approaching summer one I very much wasn't looking forward to.

Then again, had I ever looked forward to a summer with James other than the first one?

"Odette?" father called from down in the grounds.

"Oh, father," I cried, heading towards the window where I started coughing like I was going to hack up a lung and all the rest of my insides after it, "I'm sick. Can't we postpone this a week? What's losing a week when we have the whole summer?"

"You wish," said father. "Come on. Hurry. And don't forget to pack one of your best outfits, because your mother is planning on taking you, James, and perhaps his little friend Don out to a horse show for your birthday in August. Your mother went to one for her 12th birthday, too."

"I hope James doesn't fall asleep," I muttered, but father didn't hear me as I mooched off to the suitcase on my bed. "He did a few years ago when I was reading him a book about horses."

I dragged out packing as long as I could, hoping if I spent too long doing it we'd miss our boat.

Yet still, an hour later I sat, scowling with my arms folded, on the deck of the boat, watching the land disappear.

"Cheer up, Odette," said father, nudging my shoulder, "you always assume it'll be worse than it turns out to be."

"Do I?" I huffed. "It's never *good*, father."

"There are good days within it."

"The whole chunk of time by itself is bad even with those good days in it."

He pulled me close to his side. "Think about the good things that aren't Prince James," he suggested. "Remember last summer how you and Queen

Euberta started having evening tea together? Or the summer before when Bertram taught you how to conduct an orchestra? Or the summer before when you somehow—and I'm still not sure how you did it—convinced those guards to play hide and seek with you? Everyone in that castle adores you, Odette."

"Everyone except Prince James."

"You never know," said father. "Perhaps he likes you more than he lets on. Perhaps he likes you more than he lets himself *realize*."

"Doubt it," I muttered.

With a long and drawn-out sigh, father got to his feet and patted me on the shoulder. "I'll go and ask our ship chef to make you your favorite lunch," he said.

I gave it three more bursts of efforts—faking being sea sick, faking falling over board, and pretending I was allergic to travel—but then I was out of ideas. I accepted my fate. We were going, and *maybe* that wasn't so bad.

Father had a point. These trips were so focused on James for me that I tended to forget all the other positive elements. Like, there were some positives directly related to him. Like, I saw him fall in some mud once, and laughed myself silly as he screamed like a girl and ran into the castle to change.

"I hope that happens again," I told mother, when she came to check on me before bed. "It really was the highlight of last year."

"*Odette,*" mother scolded.

"What? If he's anything like the boys his age from town, he deserves it."

"I'm sure he won't be anything like them," said mother. She pushed a lock of my hair behind my ear, and I sighed. "He's still the same person he was last year. Well, hopefully a bit more mature."

"Same person as he was," I repeated distastefully. "Well, he's never been very nice. I don't understand *why*."

Mother moved as if weary, climbing into my small bunk next to me and squishing me up against the wall. I had my own grand room on the ship, of course, but I preferred sleeping on the little bunk because it was a more nautical experience. It made me feel like I was on a grand adventure, going off into the horizon and off to a new land.

"Boys are silly and complicated," said mother, laying us both down slightly. "Well, all people are. And some start out rough around the edges, and every year they grow more mature, more likely to gravitate towards people they didn't get along with at first as they find things they have in common. That's why we come back summer after summer. Eventually, you two might discover you have more in common than not, after all. Tell me, do you dislike Prince James?"

"No," I muttered, and added, "I don't *like* him, either, though. And we have nothing in common."

"But have you *tried* to discover if you have anything in common? If you tried, then maybe you'd find there's something there, after all."

I couldn't meet mother's eyes. I turned my head, but she it turned back towards her, making me giggle slightly. Her eyes were tired. Maybe as tired as me.

"Next year you'll be a teenager, you know," she said quietly, sounding as though this truly pleased her, "and that's very grown-up. So even if you don't get along with him this year, next year maybe."

"James has been a teenager for three years, and he's not grown-up," I said.

Mother laughed. "Maybe he just needs a more mature teenager to help him get there." She winced. "It should never be someone else's job to make someone into a good person, you know, but the age difference *could* be contributing to the unease. Maybe he'll start taking you more seriously when he sees you all decked out in your royal attire, when he realizes you're growing up, too. Or maybe Bertram will finally talk some sense into him. Either way, every year is another opportunity for you two to become friends."

My mind wandered back to when I first heard I was going to be visiting him and I assumed we'd be friends straight away. The more time that passed, the less likely it seemed.

"Now, sleep," said mother. She put her fingers under my chin, lifted my face, and kissed my forehead. "Have one last nightmare about how dreadful the summer will be, then wake tomorrow to realize it won't come true."

"Says you," I mumbled, but I smiled at her as she climbed out of my tiny bed, left the room, and closed the door softly behind her.

With a sigh, I shut my eyes, half wanting the morning to come sooner because at least then I'd know how the summer would start.

But mother did have a point. James probably *didn't* see me as very grown up, and that would have to change.

In the morning, I'd have to start fresh with him. Try to make his acquaintance all over again. Show him I was someone he could take seriously.

Maybe if I put in some effort, he would, too.

4

James

Why did all good things have to come to an end?

Things started out so *well*. It was weird.

This summer, Odette was nice. She offered to play my games my way. She asked me what kind of royal duties I got to complete during the nine months we were apart. She told me I looked very grown up with my hair grown out, but I didn't really believe her because Don still said I looked like an idiot.

Her lack of shoes and muddy knees didn't bother me much now she was being cordial. I wasn't sure she *liked* me, exactly, but at least she was making an effort. She wasn't just tagging along and expecting to fit in without trying.

She'd changed.

"That's not fair, James," mother scolded me. "Odette shouldn't have to change for you to take her seriously."

"Aren't you at least glad I'm trying?" I folded my arms. "I'm thinking of inviting her out riding tomorrow, a little deeper into the forest than usual, just to try and be nice."

I surprised even myself with that thought. Usually, inviting Odette somewhere was the last thing I wanted to do, but it seemed I was less averse to her than usual this year.

Mother put her hands together, shrieking with joy.

"Splendid! Oh, James, that's splendid. Yes, do that. I was going to talk to you about inviting her out to things, actually. Next year Lord Marquis is having his 60th Birthday Ball in his manor, and I was going to suggest you invite Odette to it. It would be like the first gesture of courtship. You're not quite there yet—the age difference does make that a tad tricky—but laying the groundwork, well, anything you can do will help."

Oh yes, what was that? The sound of the good things coming to an end.

Courtship! Odette was a *child*, and we weren't even friends, yet mother wanted me to *court* her? I canceled the horse ride then and there.

"Oh, James, honestly," Bertram huffed. "I've already told the stables to expect you there bright and early—they're grooming two of our finest horses as we *speak*. What *changed?*"

I shrugged. "I thought it would seem too ... *you* know. *Weird*. Close. I don't want to get *too* close to Odette."

Bertram scowled, the lines on his face making him appear even angrier.

"You're *damn* lucky I haven't told Odette to clear her schedule for tomorrow yet. You know she loves horses. She'd be devastated if you told her you were going out then pulled out so suddenly. Honestly, James, you need to start showing her a little more respect."

"I've shown her nothing but respect," I said.

"HAH!" Bertram folded his arms. "Tolerance is not respect, James."

"I know. I've *been* respectful."

"Oh yes? Then tell me why, year after year, she's come in upset that you've ditched her for Don or you've spoiled a game by getting too cocky or you've swiped all the cards off the table because you've lost your tenth game of poker in a row. *Respecting* her doesn't mean upsetting her, James."

"I— well—"

I just scowled and walked away. If Odette was upset ... well, okay, usually I'd feel bad, but today that was *her* problem. I needed a *break*. This whole *courting* mess was still stuck in my head and tainting my view of her, so I couldn't do anything about it today anyway.

After spending the day alone brooding, I sought out Ron and invited him to spend the entire *next* day in my treehouse with me instead. It was probably petty and childish, but I made a very distinct "NO GIRLS ALLOWED" sign and hung it from the main support beam.

"We have to have someone take a look at that later," said Don warily. "This thing isn't as stable as it used to be."

I looked at our old treehouse, noticing the cracks and creaks for the first time. We'd had it for 10 years, and it was in the area that attracted the most damp. We constantly had to clean it out of the corners. I'd have to have someone take a look at it after today.

"So, what's the plan for today, then?" said Don. "I thought you were going riding."

"I was," I said bitterly, "then mother annoyed me and I don't want to anymore. I deserve a day off instead."

"Of course you do. It's summer." Don reached into the sack he'd brought and pulled out a couple of turkey legs wrapped in film. He tossed me one as I settled into my usual spot in the treehouse. I had to stoop now, and it hurt my neck. The ceiling had decided to become *obnoxiously low.*

Or maybe I was taller. But today, I felt like blaming everyone and everything except myself.

I folded my arms. "Don, do you think it can work? When she grows up? This whole thing where my parents want Odette and me to get married."

Don shrugged. "Dunno. Maybe. Maybe if you were friends. *My* parents were set up and hated each other until they realized they could be friends. Then they went on, got married, and everything was fine."

Yuck.

"I always saw myself marrying a *princess,*" I huffed. "When I was a kid, I saw myself all grown up, gallant and princely and perfect, bowing to a princess in a glittery dress and asking her to dance. Then I'd picture our wedding, my coronation, and a lifetime of us doing regal stuff. You know, waving to crowds and making laws and stuff."

"Odette *is* a princess."

I scoffed. "Odette is a little girl."

"Yeah, and she's also a princess. In a few years that could be *her* in a glittery dress with you asking her to dance."

I tried to see it. I could see her face decently enough, but I couldn't make the rest work and morph into that perfect picture in my mind. It was like I needed to see it to know there was potential, but until then ...

No.

I unwrapped my turkey leg and pushed all the thoughts away. They didn't matter. Today was my day off, not a day to think about a future I'd never have if I was to marry Odette when we grew up.

Or when *she* grew up. I was *very* grown up, thank you very much. Almost 15, almost a man.

And when I was an *actual* man I could make my own choices. I could choose to ... choose too ...

Who was I kidding? Marrying Odette was best for the kingdom, so I'd end up doing it. For the kingdom.

A knock at the door drew me out of my thoughts. I peeked out the tiny window in the top of the door, but there was nobody on the ladder. It must've been the wind. I settled back down, but as soon as I did, there it was again.

This time the knocker made herself known. I winced as her little voice called up, "James?" I peered out the window this time, and looked down. She'd used a long stick to knock.

"What?"

"Queen Euberta said there was something you wanted to ask me and told me where you were."

I drew away from the window, my eyes wide.

"Mother told her what I said yesterday," I hissed. "*Ugh*. That wasn't my plan. Especially not now I've canceled it."

"Shit," said Don.

"Don't swear, Don." I returned to my knees and leaned my head out the window once again. She wasn't unreasonable. She'd get it. "Uh, no, I don't have anything to ask you. I changed my mind. Bye."

"Wait!"

Crumpling, I stuck my head back out the window. "What?"

"Can I join you?"

I raised my eyebrows. I was in here to escape her. Letting her in would be like removing a beehive from your porch then taking it into your bedroom.

"Read the sign."

Odette's eyes skimmed over the sign on the support beam. The comprehension dawned, and she rolled her eyes.

"Real mature," she said.

"A man needs his privacy," I said, slightly haughtily, raising my head. It smacked hard against the window frame and I winced, glowering as she laughed.

"You're not a man," said Odette. "You're a boy."

"I'm *almost* a man."

"You're three years away. That's a long time."

I glowered. She had a point I refused to take. Getting irritated now, I said, "Look, just go away. This is *our* day. You have to spend summers here, I know. We have to bond. But we don't have to spend every waking moment together."

It was Odette's turn to glower now. "I never said we did."

"Well, you're not going away."

"No, because your sign is stupid."

"*You're* stupid!"

Don scoffed. "Real mature."

I rolled my eyes. I didn't need my best friend quoting Odette at me.

"Your *boys only* treehouse is stupid," Odette retorted, and I saw the end before it came. She pulled back her foot and aimed before I could shout. Her toe collided with the creaking support beam—

Crack.

I should've just let her in. The hatred I felt for myself in that moment was only matched by my panic.

I didn't know which part of myself to protect. My face, obviously, and my head, but I needed my limbs. Though I did need my face and head more than I needed my limbs, so I wrapped my arms around my head and braced for impact as we crashed.

It only lasted seconds. I tumbled out, spiraling through the air, and the sickening crack of my arm bone paired with a searing, white hot pain came with the weight of Don landing on top of me, and apparently, it wasn't just me he damaged.

Odette screamed—I was on her leg. Most of the treehouse had yet to fall, then I tried to move and a shower of wood came tumbling down. A large plank landed on Odette's wrist.

"I'm okay!" Don's weight increased on top of me, making me cry out as he moved. "I'm fine. I'll ... Oh. I'll go get help."

Of course he was okay. I broke his fall.

When I moved my leg I winced violently. It wasn't broken, but there was something wrong with it.

I used my non-broken arm to pull the plank away from Odette without speaking. Then, with a mighty heave I knew I'd regret, I pulled myself off of her. Her leg lay on top of a branch and a small pile of planks, and I knew without asking it was broken or shattered.

"I'm sorry," I gasped, not sure if I was too afraid to talk or if I was in too much pain. "I'm so sorry."

I just didn't want her bothering us today. But this, *this* was the last thing I wanted, and suddenly the intensity of my beating heart matched the pain in my arm, leg, and neck.

It began to take over, dulling the pain, and now the guilt was the most agonizing thing in the world as it scorched through me like fire.

Odette stated at me, not crying, but with her eyes wide and wet and full of pain. I had a horrible feeling the pain in them wasn't down to her injuries.

"Why do you hate me so much?" she whimpered.

Hate her? I couldn't hate anyone, except maybe somebody who hurt somebody I cared about.

My mouth opened and closed like a fish out of water. There were no words to fully articulate the fact that I didn't hate her, but I just couldn't figure out how to let myself *like* her. Especially when my mother was forcing me to marry this little girl, forcing me to make gestures that just felt *wrong* because we never got along, we couldn't find any common ground, and our interests seemed to lay in different areas.

I didn't dislike having her around. I just couldn't figure out how to include her, and it irritated me, so it was probably best if she just did what *she* wanted to do while she was here.

"I—"

A death-defying shriek cut me off as mother arrived. Odette's parents and a couple of staff members weren't far behind.

"Oh, Odette you poor darling," cried mother. "Look at your leg, it's twice the size it should be! Your poor leg. Oh, and your wrist, it's inflated like a balloon ... and James. James, are you alright?"

I winced. Although our injuries were similar, I could understand why my mother panicked over Odette before me. Hers looked bad. My arm was just folded into my body, probably shattered but not broken.

"My arm," I croaked, "and I think my leg ..."

Mother let out another shriek.

As Geoffry, one of our staff, picked me up in his arms, Odette's father picked her up and cradled her close to his chest. She still wasn't crying. When

I looked towards her, she was staring at me with her question still lingering in her eyes.

I opened my mouth again, but once more, no words came out. She turned her face into her father's chest as he carried her away, far away from me.

"What did you do, James?" cried mother, her voice wobbling as she followed Geoff and I. "What have you done?"

There were three of us there. Three of us who could've been liable for that treehouse breaking and injuring two of us. Yet it was fitting that she jumped to the conclusion that this was my fault.

I was the one who hurt myself, who hurt Odette—after all, I'd apparently spent years hurting Odette more than I realized.

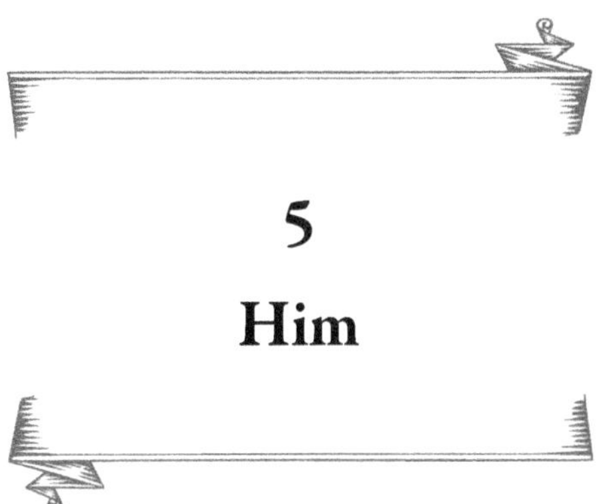

5

Him

Lord Tyrone, right-hand man to the king, commanded a minimal staff of cleaners, gardeners, and guards.

So, I was definitely startled when he ran towards the gates, shouting, "Your Majesties!" and I finally turned my attention to them.

How had I not noticed the carriage approaching, complete with royals inside?

No! This was the summer of my attack. I'd waited and watched for years to learn the summer schedule, and I was finally certain of how I could go about this without a single thing going wrong.

I would be on the throne when the monarchs returned, ready to take them down and have them surrender and be locked up forever.

Except the little girl, of course. That would be plain cruel. But then again, no child deserved to lose their parents, so perhaps I'd lock her up with them.

Maybe I'd just set them up somewhere. Keep them there under the threat of magic, but make sure they had a nice life while I ruled their kingdom in their place?

Yes, that seemed like a better plan. It was a plan that I probably should've formulated years ago, but still. I had enough on my plate. I had a castle to take over the kingdom to rule.

And I still haven't picked what I'd look like when I did it. I couldn't look like myself. Nobody was going to take a 20-year-old king seriously, and I didn't have the energy to force them to.

I had to be all mature and a little scruffy like King Richard. Or even mature and *not* scruffy like my father.

Waiting was also an option. Aging naturally so I didn't have to take on a new form.

But it had been 10 years, and I didn't want to have to wait 10 more to feel my future was secure.

That didn't matter now. I needed a new plan.

I'd never watched the castle full. I was too afraid to. I didn't want to break up a happy family, and I considered finding another kingdom, and a new castle to take over. One with a lonesome monarch or someone yet to have an heir.

But after a year travailing this landmass, I determined the there were only too places weak enough for me to reasonably expect to take over without disaster or casualties.

Plus, I wanted to use my natural powers. I couldn't push my gem too far. Not when it was working on keeping so many people alive.

I wasn't going to attack the one with the lone monarch and her son. Her son looked too snotty to feel sorry for, and she looked like she had knives in her hair and would go feral on me no matter what form I took.

King Richard? He was soft, and Queen Lithe softer, and I didn't want to *think* about their daughter. Such a sweet little ...

No. No, if I thought about her, I wouldn't go through with it.

I *had* to go through with it, and so I began to watch as the trio of monarchs trooped towards their castle.

Wait, what was wrong with the princess? Arm and leg in casts, limping everywhere with a crutch. The loud beating of my wings creating that irritating buzz made it impossible to hear what had happened, so I landed on the king's back.

"Horrible accident," said the king. "We decided it's best if Odette recovers at home. This whole thing, this match, it may not be the best idea after all. I knew the children didn't get along, but for it to end like this ..."

Oh well. It wasn't as though those two would ever make it to their wedding. Not with what I had planned.

"Shall I call the rest of our usual staff and get this place bustling back to normal?" said Lord Tyrone. "And Odette, I don't even have to ask if you'd like me to have my wife prepare you some of her best home-made ice cream to take the sting out of your injuries."

Odette smiled. "Thank you, Lord Tyrone."

"Leave the staff," said King Richard. "It wouldn't be fair to call them back after I gave them so much time off."

"Besides," said Queen Lithe, "I think it's best there are as few people around as possible. We need a quiet, relaxed summer after that ordeal."

Oh, I could've kissed her.

That was an idea ... but it was the king's blood that entitled me to the throne.

That was also an idea. Kill her, woo him. If he didn't like me as I was, I could transform.

But I'd rather kill myself than kill another living being, so with that in mind, I took flight towards the doors of the castle, staying back so I wouldn't fly around the heads of the guards by the doors and get myself swatted.

Once I landed on the wall of a hallway, high up so nobody would notice me—then lower down, because a big fat spider started making its way towards me—all I had to do was wait and reformulate.

Come nightfall, I had my plan perfect once more.

Now, to find a safe place to stay and a safe creature to stay there as ...

Honestly, sleeping in the woods as a human seemed smartest, so I flew out of the castle and curled up in a big, cushy bed surrounded by a protective shield that would hold through the night. A little clock of my own making would make noise when it was time for me to wake.

Nerves tumbled through my morning, but I couldn't let that stop me. The area was dead quiet, and guards nowhere to be seen, so I figured it was better to sneak away through the bushes and grass patches towards the entrance of the ballroom.

I crawled under the door, then buzzed my way around the castle. A moment by front doors confirmed there were guards standing outside it all day and night.

A quick sleeping spell knocked them right out, just like the ones at the front the gate before I returned to the castle and made my way around it.

I knew were all staff slept, so I began to destroy, disassembling furniture in the castle and some of the stone structure to pile the corridors with rubble they couldn't get through.

I blocked every path, thanking my lucky stars that the royals slept in in a different wing of the castle and could get to the entrance hall with ease.

I sealed every entrance with magic, windows and all, then sealed the areas I blocked off with rubble for good measure. As dawn approached, it was only a matter of time before the king rose.

Mentally, I thanked Lord Tyrone for joking, "I hope the king sleeps in instead of rising for his usual breakfast at sunrise." He let the king's schedule slip so I didn't have to dig around and find it out.

I paced as a human, cycling through appearances in a big mirror I spawned in front of me. I settled a note black cloaked gentlemen who had to be at least 40, with deep grooves in his face, bald, but with a bright red pointed beard to make up for it.

Very serious. Very mature. Harsh, and someone you couldn't say no to.

My hand constantly twitched towards my sleeve to ensure the precious gem was still there. Now, all I had to do was wait for the king to get up.

Nothing could ruin my plan.

Nothing but a knocking that made me freeze in my tracks.

This wasn't part of the plan. They weren't supposed to receive *guests*.

But there she was, knocking as clear s day, obnoxiously loud for the early hour.

"King Richard? Queen Lithe? Are you in? Somebody's been spraying perfume or bath salts or some other strange concoction at your gate, and your guards, they've been knocked out by it. Hello?"

That voice. That was a voice that could clearly carry. No!

And how did she get past my enchantments? A sorcerer didn't simply fail to produce an adequate quality spell that was so simple. I could do spells like that in my *sleep*.

"Oh dear," said the voice outside, and it was uncomfortably familiar. Even her muttering was loud enough to come through the door. "Perhaps there's trouble. Tell me there's no trouble. I'll have to ... I'll have to break the doors down!"

I almost cackled. *As if.* Even without the magic, those things were solid oak. Even *I* couldn't break them down without powers.

The doors rattled, and my urge to laugh intensified. I folded my arms and stepped back as several more heavy thuds told me what sounded like a small woman was throwing herself against them.

When the sound ceased, I broke out into a grin. Caught on, had she?

I turned from the doors to resume my pacing. Her shrill voice hadn't woken the royals so far. Thank goodness for solid oak.

A creak made me turn back towards the doors, and my jaw was on the floor. Light spilled into the entrance hall, followed by a woman with hair almost as big as her dress which ballooned around her like she'd used all the fabric in her kingdom to make her underskirts.

As we locked eyes, she stuffed a hairpin back into a half grey, half brown mane of an updo.

No way did a hairpin unlock those doors and break my enchantments. The mist that rendered those doors enchanted was still lingering in the air, yet she'd somehow stepped right through it.

"Who are you?" asked who I now recognized as Queen Eugenia Bertha of the kingdom of Wolfswood.

Well, she *had* to be knocked out. It was my only option. I fired a spell directly at her head, which she dodged.

"Well, that wasn't very nice!" she shrieked.

She dug her fists into her hips, and I blinked several times. People had never dodged my spells before. I tried again, and this time she ducked. It skimmed the top of her hair.

"You'll be hearing from my stylist and will be paying the price to fix this damage!" she snapped, pointing with a shaking finger at the singeing at the top of her updo.

I shot the spell at her in the shape of a flaming ball. She skirted around it as if she did this professionally.

"Oh, for crying out loud!" I groaned.

"Oh, so the smarmy sorcerer *does* speak! You're being very rude, you know."

I withered. "Oh, shut up."

This time she backed out and slammed the doors just as my spell hit. They flew open again and she stormed into the room as if there'd been no interruption.

What the hell was going on with her? It never took this long to take an enemy down.

We locked eyes for just a moment, then she threw back her head and *screamed*.

My eardrums wanted to kill themselves and be buried 10 feet under the ocean floor to avoid hearing that scream in the afterlife. Wincing away from it, I tossed spell after spell at her, trying to do *something* to slow her down.

When her skirt caught fire, she seized a vase and put it out. When I tripped her up, she rolled away from my next hit. This woman was more slippery than a snake covered in carriage wheel lubricant and she had the audacity to *laugh* as I groaned.

"Queen Euberta?"

Oh, well, shit.

The king and queen stood on the staircase, both with swords pointed right at me.

"My rescuers!" Queen Euberta cried.

Nobody could be as slippery as that woman. At least now I could take out the targets, lock them up, and get my plan back on track. I'd have to hit her eventually, or maybe she'd run screaming when she thought the King and Queen were dead.

I could not risk missing. I pulled back both hands, fingers clenched and shaking, power building. I needed this to hit them fast.

The king took his next step towards me as I pulled back my hands—

Everything went black.

I came to, feeling like I'd been hit by a ton of bricks. That insufferably shrill voice cackled, droning on about how she had no idea she had that strength in her as she trailed behind whoever was dragging me.

Up ahead, my eyes focused on a glow in the hands of the queen.

"No!" It came out all groggy, like I was a madman. "My gem! GIVE ME BACK MY GEM!"

My legs dragged and scratched along the floor, bound in chains as the king dragged me with him. Conscious now, I kicked out but couldn't find footing. The chain between my feet was too short.

"Give me back my gem!"

"Silence," King Richard snapped, "sorcerer."

He rattled me violently. My head smacked against the stone ground as he dragged me further, heading towards stairs. I couldn't risk getting knocked out again.

Could I escape a prison cell? Did I risk it? They'd surely see my attempt, and maybe they'd be expecting it. Or they'd kill me before they got me locked up.

There was only one way: get out when they least expected it. When they thought I was weak.

I could come back for the gem later. It was just that woman's fault. She was the one who ruined everything. Queen Euberta.

I could live a day without it. He wouldn't dispose of it, surely. Not when he knew it belonged to a sorcerer, for surely that old hag had told him everything.

There was nothing to do but transform, slipping out of my chains as my body shrunk and became feathered. I needed to be something large enough for him to see I'd escaped, so I twittered around his head before turning back into a fly and propelling myself as fast as I could go.

I hid in the castle all day, but was forced to the outside with the chaos that ensued. He had every room sprayed for bugs, forcing the queen and his daughter out of the place. He spent his day in the garden, watching.

By the end of the day his usual higher quantity of guards had arrived, and I knew that place was impenetrable. I didn't have the skill without the gem to do a mass knockout, nor the speed to do them one by one.

My entire body burst through with sobs as my separation from my gem hit harder than before, and I knew I could only afford a short period of mourning before I had to form a new plan.

At least I had 10 more years.

6

Odette

It was the crack of dawn when mother woke me and bundled me into a raggedy cloak with a hood that obscured my face.

I couldn't paint my face this time; there was no spring festival, so I'd just look silly.

This time when we headed out into town for the day, we had to keep our heads bowed and voices low.

I glanced back at the castle as we hurried down the garden path, my eyes still thick with sleep.

"What are we doing today?"

Mother fixed my hood so it covered my face a little more, casting it deep in shadow.

"We need to get out for a while. Reconstructing those walls will be noisy. I don't want you to have to listen to that all day. You'll damage your hearing before you have a chance to grow up and stand right next to loud bands as they perform. *That's* how you're supposed to damage your hearing."

I grinned up at her, my hood falling off as I did.

Right. *Heads low* as we entered the sleepy town, the sound of my crutch supporting my shattered leg the only thing that cut through the silence.

We arrived just in time for the town to be waking, but for nobody to see where we'd come from. A baker and a couple of other merchants darted out of their stores to set up exterior displays.

Deeper into the town square, near the statue of the first queen to found our kingdom, different merchants set up stalls and customers stirred.

"Have I ever told you this is my favorite market in the whole world?" mother whispered, as the sleepy day transformed rapidly into a busy affair of shoppers and stall-owners right before my eyes.

My hood slipped back as I started looking up at her, so I leaned into her instead.

"*This* is your favorite? I thought the stuff you sent away for would be. The really expensive places all over the land mass."

Mother scoffed. "Oh, please. It's all overpriced, and it's better to buy local and support businesses as needed. *That's* why it's my favorite." She reached down for my shoulder as my free arm was in a sling. "Now, come on. Stay close. Remember how easy it is to get split up in this crowd. You never know who's around, and I need to get some things for the castle before all the good stuff is gone. Don't worry; I know this is the boring part, but it won't last long. Maybe 20 minutes, tops."

She took off with me alongside before I could tell her there was no such thing as boring when we got to spend the day together.

Although it was barely past dawn, the crowd was already thicker than comfortable. My shoulder almost collided with numerous waists, a few hips, and the upper thigh of one *monstrously* tall person.

Mother navigated our path well, so none of the collisions were head-on or too jarring as she moved from stall to stall, buying whatever she needed.

That was, until she had to dash towards a stall that started calling out that there was only one of each item, and she ran so hard I crashed directly into someone my height and we landed on the stone path with a *smack*.

"I'm so sorry!" The person I'd landed on reached out and pulled me to my feet. "I'm so sorry, I wasn't looking where I was going, it's my first time here, I'm just—"

"It's okay!" My hands immediately fixed my hood, which had thankfully stayed on during the whole ordeal. "It was my fault," I insisted.

"No, it was *my* fault," said mother. "I'm sorry. I was careless. Are you alright?"

"I'm fine," said the other person. Now that I looked properly, it was a boy around my age. He hesitated. "I'm sorry again. It's my first time here. I'm just not used to ..."

"It's fine," said mother. "Please. It was *my* wrongdoing."

The boy smiled in both of our directions.

"Thank you." The smile dropped as fast as it came. "Sorry. I have to go. Um ... sorry. Bye!"

He ran off through the crowd, this time with more care.

"All sold out!" shouted the man at the table we were heading for, and mother chuckled with a sigh.

"Oh well. That's me done for the day, then. Now let's get *you* something." She looked around, then turned back to me, beaming. "There's a clothing stall over there. Oh, Odette, *please* let me buy you a dress or two. Just something very plain. Something to help you get used to wearing them more often. You'll be a teenager next year. Ready to start presenting as a princess."

I screwed up my face, but I couldn't say no to mother. I nodded and let her walk me through the crowd.

We ended up leaving with *three* dresses, identical but for the colors: pink, dark purple, and green. They were completely plain and had no frills or puffy sleeves, so I could tolerate them.

Our next stop was much more enjoyable as we stopped by an ice cream stall and headed straight to the park before it melted, stopping on a little wooden bench to watch children play in the summer sun.

"I wish I could take this off," I said, frowning as I tugged at my raggedy robe.

"So do I," said mother, "but we can't risk being recognized. We'll be swarmed. It's a good thing nobody in the kingdom knows what happened between you and James, or we'd be recognized for sure."

I glanced down at my leg and held my sling-clad arm closer to my body. My leg wasn't *that* painful anymore. I could put some weight on it, as long as it stayed in a cast and I leaned on a crutch.

"Plus," mother continued, "you know it's not safe. There could be anyone lurking in town. Dangerous people. Con artists. People who'd kidnap us for ransom if they got the chance. But as long as we keep these on and you stay by my side, we *will* be safe."

"Even from things like what happened at the castle yesterday?"

Mother put her arm around me, tightening her grip every second.

"Even from that."

From her tone in the fierceness of her hold, I believed her.

We veered away from the topic in the afternoon. Instead, mother took me to all my favorite summer festivities and food stalls.

Music played in the streets, and the members of the town mingled and shared in the summer evening festivities.

I was never here during summer, but they all seemed to have far better a time than me.

"I first visited this event a couple of years ago, and now I try to go whenever I can," said mother, as we more walked among the dancing locals and their fiery joy. "Someday I'd like to visit here again and just be myself. We could set it up, make sure everyone knows we're coming, and make sure they all know we're just normal people like them. It seems like a far distant dream now, but one day we'll do it. I promise."

I looked out at the other children, dancing barefoot without the need for heavy hoods and cloaks and robes, and I couldn't wait until that day came.

Despite being in disguise, we were able to have a good time, good conversations, and good fun. It was dark by the time we left, the streets much quieter overall but louder in some places. Shouts came from around corners and down dark alleys, louder than any words heard in the street all day, but it was overall harmless.

"Thank you for today," I said, wrapping my good arm around mother's waist before I had to seize my crutch and walk again.

The hug was difficult due to the assortment of items hanging from a belt she wore; her purchases from this morning. She must've been very strong to be able to hold them all day, as some of them looked very heavy and expensive.

That was exactly what the woman who took mother at knifepoint said, too.

It didn't seem real. All of a sudden, time slowed down. A large woman dragged mother into a dark alley, an arm around her neck so she couldn't pull away.

There was a knife to her throat, and the woman growled, "I'm going to need a certain amount of cash here before I can let you go."

"Run, Odette!"

I always obeyed what mother said, wanting nothing more than to please her and father. My legs automatically tried to follow her order, but I stood my ground.

"No, please!" I thought I was being calm, being rational towards this person, but it just came out as childish and weak. "Please, leave her alone!"

"I will," the woman growled, her face hidden in shadow, but from what I could see of her all I perceived was danger. "When mommy here gives me the money I owe. It's a rich folk like you that are the reason I'm in debt. So it's rich folk like you who'll pay for it."

Now I knew why we needed the cloaks. If they knew who we really were, even more people like this woman would take us.

"Odette, go," said mother.

"No!"

"It's not safe for you!"

"I'd listen to your mother, kid," snapped the woman.

"I'm not leaving you!"

I so wished I could see mother's face, but I could picture it in my head so clearly, staring at me with weariness she'd never looked at me with before. Wondering why it was now I chose not to obey, wondering why I didn't follow my urge to flee for my life, wondering why the aching in my chest of a heart pounding hard enough to burst wasn't enough to turn me away.

"I'll get the money," I said.

I knew where my mother kept it, and she didn't tell me not to. I pulled out her coin purse. It was terrifyingly light—the purchases, the ice cream, it all made a dent.

The knife wielding hand took the money and scoffed.

"More," she said. "This won't be enough to get you out of this, kid. I know you've got more."

I had a tiny coin purse which I handed over in turn, making the woman cackle. If she found this so funny, maybe she would let us go.

My hopes raised, my heart soaring despite still beating so hard it hurt, but the wickedness crept back into her tone almost instantly.

"That won't do," said the woman. "But I'm feeling generous tonight. You're just a kid. So, lead me to your house, and your mother here will survive."

I knew, even without mother crying out, that I could never do that. Lead this woman to the castle, and she'd kill mother right on the spot because the woman would know death was eminent the second we got to the guards at the gate.

"I'll go to my house on my own," I said. The woman laughed again, shaking mother violently. The coins jangled and dropped to the ground so she could fully put the knife up against mother's throat again, the blade grazing her skin.

"You think I trust a snot nosed little brat like you? No. You will lead me to your house, or you will watch your mother die."

She shook mother, but my mother was smart—she seized the moment of movement to push down against the arm holding her.

She twisted it, but she couldn't flip the large woman holding her. She made a run for it all the same. My feet carried me several yards ahead before I realized there wasn't a second set of footsteps echoing off the stone ground.

I turned. The woman was on top of mother, overpowering her as she tried and failed to dodge the knife that slashed down towards her face. I ran towards the pair, and the woman pushed me down. I landed hard enough for it to knock my hood off while she was still looking at me.

"Shit," the woman breathed. "Oh, shit. You're the princess. You're the fucking princess!"

Mother's head snapped towards me. "Run."

If there was any time I should have obeyed her, it was then, but I couldn't leave her. Not even to save myself. I didn't know what I could do if I stayed, but even if ... if ...

I couldn't leave her alone as the woman ripped mother's cloak off her head.

"Fuck!" She shouted again. And she shouted the word over and over every time she plunged that knife into my mother's chest, then once through her head.

Blood sprayed everywhere, all over the stone, wide and far enough to splatter on my shoes. I squealed but didn't scramble away from it. How could I move away? It was the last warmth I'd ever feel of my mother as she lay motionless on the ground.

I had to run, but my legs wouldn't carry me away.

But I supposed it didn't matter any more, did it? Because I was going to die too, and if I were to go, at least it would be alongside my mother.

The woman rounded on me, her face still shadowed, the flickering torchlight from the streets nearby barely reaching her. Even if I did survive, I'd never be able to identify my killer.

The crunch of her feet against the stone should've terrified me, but I was oddly calm. I knew I wouldn't outrun her. Her legs was so much longer than mine.

"Hey!"

I shouldn't have looked away from her, but my head snapped towards the little voice calling out to her. Whoever it was was holding his own torch, and although I'd only seen that face once before, I recognized instantly—the boy from earlier.

"Run," said the boy.

"No. I'm not leaving her."

"I'll make sure somebody finds her," said the boy. With his free hand, he pulled out a knife. He'd never be able to take down that beast. He locked eyes with me then said, again, in a voice far too menacing to come out of such a young body, "Run."

I couldn't fathom what it was, but something told me if I didn't run, I'd regret it.

I pushed myself to my feet, not daring to look back. By the time I was halfway down the street I regretted it, because now I would never know when the last moment I looked at my mother was. Even in death, a last look was better than nothing.

There were still normal shouts breaking through the night. Nobody had heard the commotion. We never even screamed.

Then, breaking through the regular sounds of night, a wolf howled—it was too wolf-like to be a dog, but too small to be a fully grown wolf.

Then, screams. They didn't sound like the screams of a little boy. Maybe he'd stabbed her in the leg and took her down. I just hoped she hadn't fallen on top of my mother.

I ran and I ran and I ran, feeling like my lungs and throat and mouth had filled with blood, tasting metal. I couldn't make it to the castle. I eventually had to stop and catch my breath, gasping for air and sobbing, both at the same time, unable to differentiate between the two. I knew I was getting close to the castle, as the forest that bordered three sides of it was off to my left.

Footsteps approached, and I knew I had to run again, but they were too light to be anyone dangerous.

I looked back, and the boy came to a dead stop.

"Are you okay?" he asked.

He was bleeding, a big ugly gash down one side of his face. It had cut right through his eye, which was still gushing blood as he held a rag to it, his knife now nowhere to be seen.

"My Gods!" I ran towards him. "Are you—are you—?"

The boy just stared at me, much too calm, and said, "My family will look after me. They'll be angry if they know I came out here, but it doesn't matter. I just wanted to see. I just wanted to help. Go home."

The boy ran into the forest. I stared through the trees after him, even though he'd been swallowed by night. After a few moments, that wolf from earlier howled again, closer now.

Dizzy, but able to breathe again, and baffled by the events of the night, I turned and ran again, and I wouldn't stop until I reached home.

7

James

Losing my father was the worst thing that ever happened to me, even though he died doing what he loved.

Finding him like that shook me.

Dead, the ghost of final last grin and the trail of his last drink still plastered on his face.

He was cold, but I thought he was sleeping. But when I shook him and shook him and all that happened was his head lolling to one side, his burned-out cigarette falling to the floor from the hand laying on the armchair, I knew something was very wrong. He wasn't just cold and in a deep sleep.

I was only seven.

I screamed so hard I threw up all over mother, then all over Bertram, and finally, I passed out.

Would telling Odette that story make me seem sympathetic, or would it make me seem like I was making this all about myself? Perhaps the tear stains on my letter making the ink run would make it seem more authentic, or maybe she'd think it was just all for show, like everything else I did.

I sent it anyway, inviting her to come here, to come back, to escape the town she had to watch her mother die in, to escape the castle some sorcerer had apparently attacked just the day before.

I couldn't help feel that her witnessing that attack, and her mother's death, were my fault. Because she only went home because of me.

"Don't be ridiculous," said mother as she cradled me, like I was a baby, because I was crying like one. "You couldn't know when you went into that treehouse that Odette was going to kick it and get herself injured. You couldn't know even then that she would go home. You couldn't know that when she went home such terrible things would happen. It's not your fault. It's nobody's. These tragedies just happen, and if you're royal, they're just a little more likely to."

I always knew there was a reason I trained and never went out without weaponry if I ventured away from the castle. I'd advise Odette to do the same.

"Anyway, I just came to tell you that we're invited to the funeral. You don't have to go."

"I want to go. The queen was nice. And it would be rude if I didn't. It's my royal duty."

Mother stepped back and squeezed my face. Her eyes were full of pride. "There's my boy. Dutiful even in the face of tragedy. Oh, come here."

Most boys my age would be opposed to being held by their mothers, but today I needed it.

The funeral affair reminded me of my father's. Some of the customs were slightly different. The queen wasn't paraded through the town in her coffin, held up and surrounded by horses.

Her coffin wasn't there at all, and the public weren't allowed to visit her in her grave. Not even other royals from around the landmass were—it was just Odette and her father, and a couple of immediate family members I didn't know.

They all spoke to me anyway and thanked me for coming, as if it was a surprise that my mother and I were there. But we had to be, not just for our royal duties, but to be there for King Richard and Princess Odette, even though the latter and I didn't get along.

"Why did you come?" asked Odette, when it was her turn to thank me.

"I couldn't not," I said. "I know what it's like to lose a parent. And I know that after my dad died, I just wanted to run away. And I did. Mother sent me to spend the rest of the year with my cousins in another kingdom. I only came back because I didn't like it there. They had ... creatures. There were fights, and it scared me, but I promise I won't let anything scare you. I won't let anything bad happen to you, if you want to come back and stay with us for the rest of the summer. Just escape. Get away from it all for a while."

She stared at me like I had seven heads, and from the hardness in her eyes I thought she'd say no. But then she smiled.

"Thank you, Prince James."

The king didn't even look at me, and he barely acknowledged mother when she extended the invitation to him. When he said nothing, she asked if he'd like us to stay with him instead, and to that he gave a shrug and stiff nod.

After the funeral, mother informed me we'd be spending the summer in Odette's castle in support of them, and to help them run things while they grieved.

"Bertram can take care of things at home," she said, "so come on. Let's get home. Pack our things. When we return, I want you to be *extra* nice to Odette."

I was already planning on it.

When we arrived at the start of our visit, we were greeted not by the king, but by his right-hand man with Odette at his side.

"The king isn't feeling up to visitors, but he appreciates your presence," said Lord Tyrone, bowing before us both. "Our staff will show you to your bedrooms. You're welcome to use any of our facilities, visit our gardens, and venture out into town if you so wish. Just let the guards know. Our home is your home until September, and any time you so wish it to be from then on."

"Shall I show you to your room, young prince?" asked a kind member of staff, smiling down at me.

I glanced at Odette, who was looking at her feet, dressed not in black, but in—to my great surprise—a plain pink dress with her hair tied back.

"Show mother, and she'll show me later," I said. "I would like to spend time with the princess."

Odette's head jerked up. "Really?"

"Really. You said you had a game room last year. And you said it was better than mine. Show it to me?"

Odette nodded, going from sombre to eager, then gestured for me to follow.

Our walk through the castle was silent. I'd never get to know this place. The castle was bigger than mine, and grander, and not so logically laid out.

Odette's game room turned out to *really* be much nicer than mine, and it looked more like a living room than anything. A great fireplace was flanked by two chairs and a couch along with a little table which, to my great surprise, rose up and expanded if you moved a series of cranks.

"For playing games when you want to sit by the fire and be comfortable," said Odette.

There was a dining table for other games, a couple of dart boards on the walls, and a little hoop with balls piled up in a basket next to it. Oh, I knew that game, but we didn't play it often my kingdom. You'd throw balls through a basket to score points. It seemed like fun.

"First one to 10 points wins?" I asked, grabbing a ball without asking.

"You're on," said Odette, although her voice lacked emotion.

I planned on going easy for her, but I found I didn't have a natural knack for the sport. She only missed one on her path to 10, but I missed four. When I groaned and threw my head back, she laughed, ending with a little giggle so quiet it was as if she was afraid to do it.

"Best-of-three?" asked Odette. "You're a guest. It's only fair I give you a shot to win back your dignity."

I put my fists on my hips. "I haven't lost my dignity. Let's do it."

By the end of the next round, I very much had lost my dignity.

I also very almost rid her castle of a little bust of a dog that apparently belonged to the king. My aim was so bad that my ball ricocheted off the wall, off the table, and skimmed that dog on the mantle.

"Maybe we won't play any more basketball today," said Odette. "Do you think you're any better at board games? I know you're terrible at cards."

I was better at board games as it turned out, though I still went easy on Odette. Either that or she was better than I thought, and I worse.

There was no going easy on her once she pulled out a deck of cards, though, and although day by day I tried to improve, I continually failed.

"Who taught you to play cards?" I asked.

"My father," Odette said proudly. "He's the only one who can beat me. He's the only one who can beat me in anything we played together. Although, I let mother beat me once, just to see her smile."

At the word, my face broke into a soft grin. It sounded like what I was doing during games I was competent at, and I did see Odette smile more often than not.

I knew how badly she was still hurting. She couldn't not be. At least I gave her a break from it, even if only for a few seconds.

"Well, I'll have to improve and become good enough to not only beat you, but your father as well."

"Oh, you'll never beat him," Odette giggled, but it died in her throat and the darkness washed over her. "I'm not sure I ever will again, either."

"What do you mean?"

"He hasn't come out of his room in days. He's barely even talking to me. I guess he's just really sad. He wants to be alone. I'll respect that. But I miss him."

Miss him? Odette probably did more than that. When my father died I couldn't leave mother's side. I needed to be near her, because she was the only one who loved my father as much as I had.

We helped each other through our tragedy, but Odette? All she had was me to distract her, and mother doing her best, too. This morning she had tea with mother and they had another afternoon tea planned after our daily gaming ritual.

It should've been the king. He was the one who was supposed to protect his daughter from harm, and he of all people knew what she was going through.

"Let's not talk about it," I said, not wanting to brush her off, but not wanting to upset her further. "Let's ... Well, we haven't been outside in days. Let's go out. I saw you have gardens—"

"No. Mother and I used to go there."

"Alright. Well, let's go look at the horses. I know you like horses. And do you have any training grounds?"

Odette nodded, and so we left the castle to seek distraction elsewhere.

We spent so long patting and grooming the horses—well, I watched—that by the time we got inside and washed up, it was time for her afternoon tea with mother.

"You're welcome to join us, James," said mother. "It's not just for ladies."

That actually sounded nice. I opened my mouth to accept her invite, but I shook my head and different words came out.

"I ... I kind of want to go down to the training grounds. Keep up my practice."

"Very well, have fun. Come, Odette. You simply *must* tell me about that book you mentioned this morning. I couldn't find it in your library. Then again, you know the library better than I do."

Mother and Odette made their way down the corridor and off into a little private dining room. They'd be in there for at least an hour, giving me ample time to carry out a plan that, while watching Odette, I'd been unconsciously forming.

I didn't know the way fully, but had a rough idea of where the royal bedrooms were.

It wasn't that hard to find my way. The increase of guards along the corridors was a pretty good giveaway that the king was around here somewhere. I knew I was in the exact right place when two guards stopped me from entering a corridor.

"What's your business here?" asked one.

"Princess Odette wanted me to get something out of her bedroom," I said. I didn't know anything she owned. Well, apart from something she probably didn't still have, something I gave her when she was a baby. Would they know if she still had it? "She asked me to go get her heart cushion. She'd like to use it tonight when we resume our games. We have a long board game planned, and—"

"Oh, go ahead, then," said the guard. "But be quick. King Richard is just a few doors down, and we don't want any noise disturbing him."

"Of course."

Well, that was easy.

The corridor was obscenely long. It split off to the left and right, with doors on either end of these walkways. I assumed one was Odette's, and the other belonged to the king. One had guards in front of it, so I turned down that path.

"Excuse me?" I said, putting on my most angelic voice, that of a perfect young prince who meant no harm.

"Oh, are you lost, young prince?" asked the guard on the left. "Not to worry, I can tell you how to get out of here. Take the—"

"Actually, ma'am, it's urgent, but all the guards in the castle are needed in the ballroom immediately. It's an emergency. I was sent here to make sure nobody bothers the king while you're gone."

The guards exchanged a look.

"What kind of emergency?"

"That man. He's been spotted. The sorcerer. They want all hands on deck just in case something happens. Mother doesn't want the king to worry, so you shouldn't go bother him about it or anything."

This time when they exchanged a look, it was one of urgency. I had to be urgent too, since as soon as they met the other guards they'd know I'd lied.

They warned me not to disturb the king. I nodded and waited until they were out of sight before I slipped inside.

"I told you to knock before you entered," King Richard said dryly, and I squinted through the darkness to see him.

We appeared to be in a grand room, but the curtains were drawn. A bed sat unmade but empty against the wall opposite the door. The sound seemed to come from somewhere to my left. There was a large sofa in the sound's vicinity, with a hunched figure sitting with his head bowed.

"Your Majesty," I said, "I'm sorry. I know I shouldn't have disturbed you, but—"

The king turned. I was glad for the darkness, because he appeared more haggard even in shadow than I'd ever seen him. I could tell even in this dim light that his face was creased in anger.

"Prince James," said the king. "You shouldn't be in here. I asked not to be disturbed. I don't want—"

"To talk to anyone? Neither did mother when father died. But you can't hide in here forever." I wanted to approach, puff out my chest, but something about his grey-faced glare kept me in my place. "You can ignore me. You can ignore mother. You can ignore all your guards and your lords and nobles. But Odette needs you right now."

Something in his face changed, but I couldn't tell in this light if it was for the better. There were four sets of footsteps in the hall already.

"You're the only one who understands what she's going through," I rushed. "Nobody can comfort her but you. If there was ever a time she needed you most, it's now."

The door burst open. A guard's hand was on my shoulder within seconds.

"You're not allowed to be in here, young highness," she said sternly. "You're coming with me."

I wouldn't resist. I turned back to the king one final time as the guard attempted to walk me out.

"Think of her, your Majesty," I said. "She shouldn't be alone."

I turned away to accept my fate as the guards walked me right to my mother.

"You shouldn't have done that, James," mother groaned as she took me away from the guards and steered me to the guest wing of the castle, grounding me there until further notice. "But I suppose your heart was in the right place. Still, it was a silly thing to do. A *very* silly thing to do."

I shrugged. "Doesn't matter. I think the *king* is the silly one, since it doesn't seem to have worked."

When I got to my bedroom, I slumped on the couch and mirrored the king, sulking away. Mother didn't say when I could come out.

Pacing, making paper boats and flying things, and picking out clothes for the next week got boring fast. Just when I was about to give up and return to the couch, there was a knock on the door.

"Come in."

It only opened a crack. Odette slipped in, her eyes on the floor. The gratitude in her face made me uncomfortable, and I didn't know why.

"Thank you for doing that, James," she whispered.

"It was nothing," I said, trying to keep away a frown as I turned away from her, unable to meet those innocent, pained eyes. In them, I saw what I felt when I lost my father so many years ago.

"Well, thank you anyway," said Princess Odette, and I brushed her off again, muttering so low she probably couldn't even hear.

"You're a lot nicer than you let on, you know," she said, and once again I couldn't meet her eyes because I wasn't sure it was true. Sure, I was being nice now, but she still spent several summers hating my guts and this hardly made up for it.

"It was the least I could do," I said, my eyes firmly on the wall opposite her.

"Father asked me to have dinner with him in his room. And he's reinstating our nightly walks that we always took during the summer, before we started staying with you."

"Good for you."

"I was wondering if you'd like to join us."

"Can't," I said, "being punished."

I still wasn't sure why I was uncomfortable, or why I was being so short with her. Maybe it was because the look on her face made me want to go over there and give her a hug or something, and that was definitely something we didn't do, so I had to keep my distance.

But I couldn't be rude. So, I looked at her and said, "also, I'm writing a letter to Don. He's probably going insane without me. So ... yeah."

Odette appeared crestfallen, but I knew she was probably relieved. Maybe her father told her to invite me as a thank you, to be polite. She'd never ask me of her own accord.

"Okay. Well, enjoy that, then. I'm going to go. See you."

"Yeah, whatever." I turned from her again. I needed to give her a break from having to look at me without rolling her eyes the way she usually did. I knew she wouldn't be able to resist the urge to scoff at me for long.

By the time I turned back, she was gone. Good. The only person she should've been with was her father, so I continued to take my punishment.

Now I didn't really mind doing the time. It was worth it since the king had apparently taken my words to heart.

8

Odette

"Two years later and you still haven't taken my advice."

James lowered his cards and brow simultaneously.

"Your advice?"

"Don't you remember? Two years ago—the summer after the one you spent at my castle—I wrote you a detailed plan for how you could rearrange this room and make it far more appealing and more logically laid out. As it is, it's a mess. It's hard to get through it."

James put his cards face down on the table. "I thought you just said that because you wanted to annoy me."

"Oh, I did, but I also think this room could do with some serious rearranging. Like, seriously, those dart boards, there's no room to get far enough back to feel proud of yourself when you hit something. And that pool table, the pool cues keep knocking against the wall. And it makes no sense to have the card table all the way over here in the dark corner when come nightfall, we can barely see our cards."

James rolled his eyes. "Well, it's not my room to rearrange. It was my father's. And he didn't use it for anything very logical. He only really used this table, and he used candles to see his cards. The other stuff in here was mostly just for show. Nobody's touched it since he died in it."

My eyes dropped to my cards, and I couldn't see them any more with the guilt that coursed through me.

"Sorry. I didn't know."

"It's not that I can't tolerate— or, I mean, it's not that I don't want to because it was his anything," said James. "It's just that I think it's fine as it is."

He glanced towards the dartboards and pulled a face that told me he was lying. I rolled my eyes.

He was always lying, I was sure of it. Any time he showed an ounce of sincerity, he pulled back. If he ever complimented me or told me I did a job well done on something we did together, he acted like he hadn't said it two minutes later.

His good moods lasted about as long as the ceasefire in the nation that had been in two separate 100-year wars in 200 years.

Clarence entered the room with a tray to take our empty drinks. Ugh. I'd never get another drink in good time with *him* working.

Unless I used a little trick I learned from a book on how to charm people to get them to do whatever you wanted.

"Oh, wow. Clarence? Is that you?" I batted my eyelashes at him.

He paused. "Yes, YourHhighness."

"I hardly recognized you. Is that a new haircut?"

"It is, Your Highness."

"It suits you. And did you have your uniform altered? Because it seems to hug your biceps so *well*." I bit my lip, then smirked. It all felt very inauthentic, but the red blush creeping up his neck showed my plan did exactly what I wanted it to do.

"Thank you, Your Highness. Is there ... is there anything else I can get you once I take your empty drinks away? I'll come right back with it."

I was still waiting on that water I asked him for two years ago. He said he'd "get around to it."

"An iced apple juice would be divine. Oh, and I suppose, these two ...?"

"I'll have a beer," said Donald. He grinned. "I love being 18. You know, James, when I was your age—"

"If you tell another story about something you did two weeks ago, I'll ban you from this castle," said James, through gritted teeth.

I tried not to laugh. James would be 18 in three day's time. Donald seemed to be milking his elder status for all it was worth until then.

"And you, Prince James?" said Clarence.

"Nothing," said James glumly.

Clarence turned back to me with a gracious smile. "Your drinks will be here momentarily, young princess."

I let out a high laugh and began twirling my hair around one finger.

"Oh, thank you, Clarence. Thank you."

I relaxed my posture. Maybe I didn't have the perfect hair or fancy dresses to get people riled up when I wasn't performing royal duties, but I was like a sponge. If I read about something, I'd never forget it.

"What the hell was that?"

I turned towards James. "What do you mean?"

"You're 15—"

"I'm almost 16."

"You're 15 and you're flirting with him. That's not right."

I scoffed. "Oh, please. He knows you're my betrothed. He knows I'm underage. But it doesn't matter. If someone with a pretty face says pretty words, men will bend to their will. And many women, come to think of it. And that person who works in our armory who's neither."

"That doesn't make it right," said James.

He scowled at me like I'd done something against him personally. It made me want to fold my arms, turn away and hide my face.

Father thought it was hilarious the other day when I took the flirting approach with Lydia, the one who always forgot to put the ice in my juice.

Queen Euberta had patted my shoulder and said, "Look at you. You're growing up so well."

But of course, nothing could please James. He was so nice when I arrived, but he withdrew further with every second we spent together.

Just another normal summer with James. His nice front *never* lasted. He hated me and I knew it, so why did I even try to be nice to him or speak playfully when I could just buy into his dislike, too?

Every time he did something kind for me, he always reverted to a state of dislike shortly after. Like when he got my father to send for me after weeks of silence when my mother died. He was quiet for the rest of the summer, and the next year he acted like it had never happened.

He was never outright mean to me, but he didn't seem to want to know me very much, either. He was so rigid. So uptight about how he wanted to present himself to me, to the world.

It was like he was afraid to show me he was a real person.

"Let's just keep playing," I muttered, tearing myself back to the present. "Who wins this round?"

"Probably you," James muttered.

For the sake of the tension between us, I hoped it wasn't me.

Thankfully, Donald was the winner. That, at least, got me a little leeway to compliment the tightness of Clarence's pants when I developed a craving for some of Chef Quince's homemade cupcakes which I knew he'd be making today for my afternoon tea with Queen Euberta.

"Oh, I'll bring you one, Your Highness," said Clarance, leaving me grinning right at James's scowl.

"You really need to stop doing that," he said.

"No," I replied crisply. "I'll stop when we're married. *If* we get married."

At this rate I didn't think it was ever going to happen, but I had to keep trying. Mother would've wanted it. It was best for our kingdom.

The rest of our gaming session past mostly in silence. When I left James and Donald to their own devices, I didn't even bother saying much of a goodbye. I had a far more enjoyable matter to attend to as I sat down across from the Queen for afternoon tea.

"Oh Odette, I'm so glad you enjoy doing this with me," said Queen Euberta, beaming as she poured our drinks and served cakes. "James always enjoyed it when he was young, but ever since his father died, well, he's been too obsessed with wanting to seem busy and like everything he does had some kind of royal purpose. He has no time to spend with his dear old mother."

"I think you should always find time to spend with your mother," I said. "And with one as wonderful as you, he's definitely a fool."

She gave me an impish smile. "I don't want to seem like I think too highly of myself by saying that you're right, but when the shoe fits ..." She grinned at me, and we shared a laugh. Hers died away and was replaced by a weary sigh. "How is he, then? James? Is he behaving himself?"

It seemed silly to bring up the little argument we'd had because it was over, so I just shrugged.

"He's the same as usual."

"Oh, well, I'm not sure that's a good thing," said Queen Euberta, chuckling. "But I suppose it's better than him being rude or something."

I gave her a wry smile. Sometimes I wished he *would* just be outright rude to me—it would be better than living in a constant state of not really knowing where we stood.

I concentrated on my tea, staring at the dark liquid in the cup. Despite its darkness, the light in here made it so I could see right through it, down to the bottom of the china.

If only I could see through James the same way.

"What's the matter, dear?" asked the Queen. "You are telling the truth, aren't you? He isn't being ... well, *overtly* unpleasant, is he?"

I shook my head, but my worries made their way out anyway.

"Why doesn't he like me?"

I sounded so much more pathetic than I'd intended.

Queen Euberta gave me a sympathetic smile as she placed a hand on my shoulder. It wasn't sympathy I wanted. It was a genuine answer I sought.

"Oh, James is just stubborn," Queen Euberta chuckled. "He'll come around. He likes you, really. He really does. He asks about you in the weeks coming up to your arrival. He always reads the latest news from your kingdom, particularly if it involves you. Trust me, Odette, James likes you a lot more than he lets on."

I wasn't so sure, but I didn't want to tell her. I just gave a little smile and said, "Thanks. I guess so."

The thought that he liked me in secret wasn't as comforting as she probably thought it was. If he was ashamed to like me, then that was probably worse. It meant there was something *wrong* with me, and that thought cycled through my head throughout the rest of our usually enjoyable afternoon tea.

9

James

"Odette and James sitting in a tree, K-I-S-S-I-N-G. First comes hatred, then arranged marriage, then ... I mean, probably a baby, but that's too scary to put in rhyme."

"What the hell are you talking about?"

I rounded on Don with my arms folded as we got up from the card table. Somehow it wasn't quite as fun as usual, even though Odette wasn't here to beat us any more. I didn't really like being in this room without her, even if my best friend was here with me.

"You like her," said Don. "Fess up. You *like* her. That's why her flirting with the staff bothers you so much. You complain about her bad attitude and her constant refusal to dress like a princess even though her being here is technically classed as a 'royal duty', but you can't deny it. You like Odette, James."

We left the game room, heading outside. Now Odette was with mother, I wasn't sure how to fill my time.

"Don't be ridiculous," I scoffed. "I just don't think she should flirt with guards when she's so young. Or with a*nyone*."

"Except with you?"

"Absolutely not. No. That's ... that's even worse. Anyway, she never would."

"Alright. She never would, and you wouldn't want her to, and I totally didn't catch you staring at her and the king going for a walk through the grounds that the other day, with hearts in your eyes."

"I was admiring the king's new clothes!"

"You were admiring the king's daughter, but okay. You've never been a good liar, James."

I turned towards Donald as we left the castle. "The list of reasons to ban you from this place grows every day, you know."

"I know. But you never would. Who's going to be your best man when you marry her?"

I spotted Bertram sitting on a low pillar and reading just outside the door.

"Bertram," I stated.

"Good choice," said Bertram, without looking up.

"Yeah, sure," said Don.

We wandered aimlessly. I awaited Odette's return. Maybe she'd want to go back to the game room after she finished her tea with mother, though with how I treated her earlier, it didn't seem likely.

Plus, she generally disliked me anyway, so what was the point in forcing her into yet another pointless gaming session where she'd just win everything anyway?

Donald dropped the subject of Odette as we made our way towards the training grounds for a little archery. He was still terrible, as usual, but at least he wasn't snapping the bow in his face any more. We spent the afternoon feeling proud of ourselves as I hit every target he told me to aim for. He also told me what distance to shoot from and what angle to use. I almost always got a bull's-eye.

"I tell you, James, it's a shame you're going to be king, because you'd make a really good archer."

I grumbled. "If only I could hit the bull's-eye every single time."

"You should loosen up, Your Highness," said my old trainer. "Stop being so rigid. That's how you hit it *every* time," He was training one of the young lords who lived by castle, and hadn't offered me much insight in years as I was good enough to practice alone now.

"Yeah, loosening sounds like a good idea in a lot of ways," said Don. "You haven't been loose a day in your life."

"That's not true," I scoffed. I was plenty loose—I just liked to be responsible, too.

"Yeah, right," said Don. "You're so uptight you can't even admit to yourself when you might be starting to like the woman that you have to marry in a few years."

"Girl," I corrected.

"Now. But she'll be a woman one day, and your wife. Also, is that you admitting you like her?"

"I—"

I lowered my bow. There across the grounds, Odette and her father were walking again, among the bushes that, come nightfall, were dotted with fireflies that illuminated Odette in the moonlight when she and her father took the same walk every night.

It was a little early in the day for them to be doing it now, and I watched them pass, my brow furrowing. Odette looked upset. Was it something I'd done? She disliked me intensely so I doubted it, and I tried to force myself not to care, because why should I care about someone who disliked me? Yet still I found myself wondering.

"Okay," I said, more to myself than to Don, "Maybe I like her a little. But I shouldn't. I've made her hate me and it's too late to change myself now. So I just have to keep keeping her at a distance. There's no point in changing things up after so long."

"There's always a point, James," said Don, "you're just too rigid to see it."

I aimed at the bull's-eye of the farthest target and hit just to the left of it. I groaned.

"Loosen your grip, James," my old trainer commanded. "I swear, it's the only problem I've ever had with training you."

I watched as the young boy he was training now practiced his aim and hit the edge of his target. His form needed work, but mine was perfect.

But then I supposed there was no such thing as perfection.

I loosened my grip. The next time I aimed for the farthest target, I hit it dead on center.

"See? Loosening up and can be a good thing," said Don. "So maybe if you just loosened up and let yourself be a little freer in general, you'd realize that it's never too late to change your ways. You'd realize that you can totally just go up to Odette, apologize for how you've acted for years, and tell her you'd like to try get along properly from now on."

Odette and her father passed by again, taking their nightly route of walking up and down. My eyes followed them, and Don was probably watching me but I didn't care.

I tried to picture myself going up to Odette, asking her to start again. I felt like I'd reached out in ways that would *imply* that was what I wanted over the years, yet it never worked. Something in me always snapped and I returned to just brushing her off and shrugging.

Maybe it was because I was so rigid. Maybe I just couldn't bring myself to be ... better.

"Okay." I lowered my bow and turned to Don. "Since you seem to be the expert, how exactly do you propose I loosen up?"

"By talking to—"

"Not yet. Give me another plan. What's one thing you think I'd never do? Because I'll do it. Other than the Odette thing."

Don raised his eyebrows. "Well, you refused to let me buy you a drink at The Secret Bar on my birthday. You wouldn't even celebrate my 18th with me? Every other underage guy in that place let me buy them drinks. And you're the prince. So, you know, the barman would care even less if it was you."

I rolled back my shoulders and automatically snapped into the response I'd automated at this point.

"It's unbecoming of a royal to break the law just because they're a royal."

"See? There's that uptightness I was talking about. And would you stop staring at her? If she catches you, she'll be terrified."

I turned my head from Odette's gentle gait and sighed.

"Alright. I'll let you buy me a drink. But just one."

"Well, it's a miracle."

"And I'll be wearing a disguise."

"Of course you will." Don sighed. "Okay, well, that's better than nothing I guess."

The kid my trainer was training hit a bull's-eye. He screamed, joy in his eyes. That was how I reacted to my first time doing it, too. I'd almost forgotten what novelty was like.

I was so busy with keeping up appearances that I never let myself experience anything new. Experiencing the same old, same old, was safe and expected.

Don and I made our way towards the gardens and the castle. I would need to make some excuse to mother. Well, I could probably tell her I was going out with Don, actually, without specifying what I was doing. She'd probably encourage the truth were I to confess it, but I didn't want to.

"What about the other thing I convinced the boys do?" asked Don, giving me a great big grin as we reached the castle doors. "That was a little more fun then getting them all drunk. And *very* educational."

Bertram, still reading on his pillar, snorted.

My cheeks flushed. Don's father had a habit that let him enjoy the services of a *certain type of establishment* without being unfaithful to his wife.

For the right amount of money, *a certain type of woman* would let you watch as she engaged in *a certain type of activity* with her paying customers in the *certain type of establishmen*t, and it was a *certain type of viewing experienc*e I couldn't fathom letting anyone know I'd had, were I ever to have it.

Only the people I trusted most would ever know, and that was me, me, Prince James, and that guy in my mirror.

"Absolutely not," I said.

"Oh, come on."

"No! I don't want to be seen in one of those places."

"You'll be in disguise!"

"Okay, I don't want to see the inside of one of those places."

Don snorted. "Liar. Every teenage boy in this town has fantasized about sneaking in the at least once, most of them have tried. You're just too noble and uptight." He brought us to a halt. "Two drinks. If you're not gonna do that with me, then you're going to let me buy you two drinks."

"I'll tell you what, Donald," I said, throwing my shoulders back, "I'll let you buy me three drinks if you never try to get me to do that thing again."

"Four."

"Four only if you stop bothering me about liking Odette."

"You're on."

I stuck out my hand, and Don gave it a hearty shake. Such a stupid agreement. Going out drinking when I was underage, just to prove that I could loosen up and be free.

I had to admit, the prospect of this novelty gave my heart a little jolt, but the excitement was nowhere near as prevalent as the nerves that filled my stomach for the evening looming ahead.

10
Odette

A rustling in the bushes startled me from where I kneeled in the damp summer night grass. Calming myself, I had to remind myself it was only the wind, or perhaps another little animal like the rat I'd been watching shuffle among the flowerbeds for the last hour.

I always missed my garden in summer. I missed the benches and the pond and the elegantly carved bushes forming the shapes of people and objects.

The grounds here weren't nearly as nice, and they didn't offer any coverage to anyone looking out a window. Anyone inside could see me, but I didn't really care. The only hidden spot was over there by the rustling bush.

Another shuffle, louder this time, told me perhaps this was a much larger creature than a rat—and the appearance of a familiar face, half hidden beneath a haggard hood, confirmed that seconds later.

"James?"

He looked confused, and a mess, with a stain all down his front and his hair sticking up.

James's eyes widened a moment, then he spread his arms wide.

"Odette! Hey! You're not supposed to be out here. This is my sneaking in spot. I don't usually sneak in this late. And usually I just sneak out to go sit in the woods and think about things I can't think about in the castle because I get all ... like this... like this weird pressure in my brain and it goes like ..."

He put his hands each side of his head and made a big gesture like an explosion, followed by a noise. He stumbled towards me, and I caught a whiff of something I only smelled very lightly on my parents at special occasions.

"James, are you drunk?"

"No," said James. He hauled himself up, then snorted. "I only had ... this many drinks." He held up all his fingers. "It was only supposed to be one and then two and then three and then four but Don kept coming up with excuses to let him buy me more because I wouldn't go watch the sexy ladies with him and because I didn't want to sneak off tomorrow into town in disguise with him and because we wanted to play a drinking game and because ... because... I can't remember the other reasons, but they made sense at the time."

He swayed dangerously side to side. I reached out for him, but he caught his balance and began tilting his head side to side instead as he continued.

"Why are you outside? You don't come out alone. You and the king just stroll up and down and up and down and up and down with the fireflies and the moon and ... the talking."

Had he been watching me? I didn't know whether to be concerned or flattered. It didn't matter, though, as we had to get inside now. I couldn't let the queen see him in this state.

"Come on," I said, shuffling forward to seize him under the arms. We never touched, yet now all his weight was on me. It was odd, uncomfortable, but necessary. "What's *wrong* with you? How did you ... Why did you ...?"

"Because Don said I like you and I won't tell you that I like you because I'm too stuck up and rigid, so I had to show him I'm not stuck up and rigid."

Stumbling through the garden barefoot while trying to support a near-grown man was not a task I ever wanted to do again. Strong as I was from helping out in the stables at home, I was used to wielding heavy objects and slamming them down, not carrying them across the garden.

"You got drunk because Donald accused you of liking me?"

My heart fluttered at the thought. Clearly, Donald was insane.

"Yeah. Oh, no, that probably sounds really offensive, but I promise it's not because I wanted to forget what he said or anything. I just wanted to prove a point. Also, I guess it doesn't matter if I offend you, because you hate me anyway."

We were just through the nearest doors of the castle when I had to pause, partly because he was heavy, mostly because his words were.

"I don't hate you," I said. "I mean, I don't particularly like you," I added, "but that's because you're exceptionally annoying and you don't like me, anyway."

"No," said James, stumbling away from me waggling his finger. "No, no. No ... What am I saying no to?"

"Just come on."

He seemed to have his balance back so I didn't hold onto him again. Instead, I grabbed his sleeve and began dragging him towards the stairs in the entrance hall.

I didn't know were his exact bedroom was, but I did know the general direction of it, and I assumed he was smart enough to get the message once we reached the royal wing.

"Oh." He spoke as if he'd had an epiphany. "Oh, I remember. Yes. I was saying no to not liking you. I don't not like you, Odette. You just don't like me so I ... I think I just ... try to keep you not liking me because I can't just suddenly change, you know? Because I make—" he hiccuped, "—might make you not like even more. I don't not like you, Odette. Can I tell you secret?"

His footsteps were incredibly heavy on the stairs. He seemed to be holding up okay.

"Fine," I said. I didn't have time to digest the fact that he didn't dislike me—that was a plus, at least. All this time, I got the feeling he just viewed me as a problem, one he wanted to get out of his life.

"I like you a little bit," said James, then he laughed. "Don thinks I *like* like you more than a little bit. But I don't know if I think what Don thinks. As I try not to think about that. I don't know why. Maybe because I'm scared to actually like you properly because it will feel weird because we were kind of forced into it and I don't like being forced to do things. I like to choose to do things, you know? The right things. And I guess the right thing would be to *like* like you, but the childish part of me wants to go against that anyway. You know what I mean?"

I didn't want to take him to his room anymore. I want to stop right here and slap him silly and asking what he meant. So he didn't dislike me, but he didn't want to like me because ... of pettiness?

In truth that did make me dislike him a little bit, yet the fact that he was fighting part of himself to keep that up made me want to find out more.

"I understand what you said," I stated, "but I'd rather not discuss it with you now since your brain isn't working properly and you're slurring and repeating your words and it's the middle of the night. Maybe ... we can talk about it in the morning?"

I folded my arms tightly, and he mimicked me. His clumsiness almost made me smile, but I forced out an eye roll instead.

"That sounds better, actually," said James. "I could never talk to my father when he was drunk. And towards the end, he was drunk a lot. The Drunken King, the staff called him. Bertram would *yell*, but they did it anyway. They weren't wrong."

We were getting into the territory of things I knew he'd never say sober.

"Well, don't do this again so you don't end up with the nickname The Drunken Prince."

Another set of stairs. James was getting slower at them, and I wanted more and more desperately to get him to bed so I could run away and be alone with my thoughts. Thankfully, he didn't answer me.

Come morning we had to have a serious talk. The kind of serious talk that adults typically had, ones who were in relationships. I'd read lots of books about that, about couples who weren't getting along pretending to start over from scratch, and I felt like that was something James and I desperately needed to do. Maybe I still saw him as that petty little boy who never liked me and was too obsessed with his royal duties.

Then again, he hadn't changed much, had he? But I probably hadn't either.

It wasn't a long stretch to finally be in the vicinity of his bedroom. One of these doors was his, and I was sure he could find it on his own. I stood back.

"Here we are. Go to bed, James, and drink a lot of water. Father always drinks a glass of water for every drink he has at parties. It helps you not have a hangover in the morning. I'll talk to you in the morning, alright?"

James nodded so hard it turned into a bow. I hid a laugh behind my hand as he stumbled to one of the doors and leaned against it.

"You know, you're kind of nice when you want to be," said James.

"Yes, I know. It's a shame you rarely make me want to be nice."

"Yeah. I'll try to change that. Goodnight. Don't tell my mother about this?"

"I wouldn't dream of it."

Instead of thanking me, he just grinned, and stumbled into his room. The door clicked harder than it usually would, and I was free.

The ordeal tired me too, so I headed to bed. The rat I'd been watching was probably gone now anyway.

Part of me wanted to think through everything James had said—about how he liked me but he didn't want to, but it just seemed so complicated, so messy, so unimportant.

We wasted so many years just *tolerating* each other over the summer, spending three months out of the year together but never growing closer, never maturing.

It was time for a change, but if I continued that train of thought I'd be up all night.

I let that be an issue for the next day. When I woke it was still on my mind like I'd never slept.

At breakfast, James had his head in his hands and lied, saying he'd slept funny.

"I don't actually remember how I got to bed anyway," said James. "I was so tired I just ... totally blanked on most of last night."

"I've had nights like those," chuckled Queen Euberta. "Often before a big event. Like your upcoming 18th Birthday Ball, for example. Oh, it's going to be huge. My little prince becoming an adult. And in just two short years..."

Queen Euberta let out a shriek. James winced. He hadn't taken my advice about the water, then. I tried to catch his eye and offer him a look of sympathy as part of my new pact to be nicer to him, but he wasn't looking at me.

The rest of breakfast was quiet. Nobody seemed to question James's "neck ache" or unquenchable thirst. When our parents asked us what we were doing today, we shrugged.

"I might go read," I said. "Spend more time trying to see what's different in your library to ours. So far we seem to have a lot of the same copies of books, so I'd like to see if you've got anything we haven't."

I didn't really like other libraries, even the one here. They were unfamiliar and odd, not a little safe haven like the one back home.

"I might stay inside," said James. "Spend some time in the game room."

He glanced at me. Was that supposed to be an invitation? It was a weak one that made me roll my eyes. I must've been going insane, because James looked like he smiled.

"I might take a book there," I said, nonchalantly. "The chairs are nicer than the ones in the library."

"Oh, yes," said the queen, "I've been meaning to change out those library chairs. They're horribly stiff. Bertram is always studying there, and he can't stand up without groaning for days after it. Although personally, I think it's down to his age."

"What a nice morning greeting," said Bertram, slipping into the room with a pot of tea. "I need not mention I'm two days younger than you, Your Majesty."

We all chuckled politely, although doing so looked as though it made James want to puke. I bit my lip to stop from laughing harder.

We disbanded shortly after breakfast. James didn't talk to me as we left in the same direction, but he gave me a nod. His wince made it clear any head movement was a mistake.

It seemed my plans for the day were settled—get a book that I probably wouldn't get to read because of James. I ventured into the library tentatively, greeted Bertram who was already sitting at a table reading a thick volume covered in dust, and made my way through the shelves.

What did I feel like learning about today? Well, I supposed the customs of James's kingdom was a good a topic as any. There were so like ours, but the differences, though minor, were stark.

I reached the game room. James was already sitting there, head resting on his arms with a glass of water next to him. I sat across from him.

"How are you feeling?"

"Like someone cut off my head, made it into an endless cave, screamed into it, then screwed it back on," said James.

"And do you remember why you feel like that?"

James rose like a zombie from the grave. "Because my best friend is an evil mastermind who tricked me into getting drunk when I initially only agreed to one drink."

"And do you remember why you agreed to that one drink in the first place?"

James opened his mouth, faltered, and closed it. "Something about proving I'm not stuck up," he said eventually. "I don't even know if it worked. I don't remember anything from last night. I think I remember seeing you? Were you outside, or am I going insane?"

A heavy feeling came over me, settling in my chest. It felt an awful lot like disappointment, but that couldn't be right. What did I care if he remembered the night before or not? It wasn't like we had some deep, meaningful conversation. I mean, his confession had been on my mind all morning, but wasn't exactly a big one. *Kind of* liking someone wasn't exactly something to start celebrating over.

"Yeah. I met you outside, and I got you up to your bedroom."

James winced. "I didn't say anything stupid, did I? My ... my kingdom's Lords always say really stupid things when they're drunk."

I could either be truthful or pretend he hadn't said anything at all. I decided on a third option: facetious.

"You didn't say anything *stupid*."

"Oh, good. I guess it was all garbled nonsense? Probably about the giant moose head over the bar. Oh, it was so big. Moose are like ... so big." He put his head on the table again. "I think my brain is still struggling to come back to its normal level of functioning."

So he really remembered nothing. A giant moose head was more memorable than the conversation he had with me.

"Yes, well, so they say," I said. "Larger than family carriages, I've heard. But I'd rather not discuss the size of moose. I have a book to read, so if you don't mind ..."

James waved a hand dismissively, then turned all of his attention to the glass of water.

I opened my book, wondering why I chose this one and if it was to try and seem impressive. The conversation I planned on having with him died in the back of my mind as the boring introductory pages of the book started spewing words at me.

Oh well. The conversation probably wasn't that important anyway.

11

James

I'd been to balls before, but this was way too extravagant. Hand painted banners of my face hung all over the hall. I didn't look good. My face was okay, but it only just occurred to me that my hair was exceedingly weird looking, and my expression was dead.

"Nonsense," said mother, patting me on the shoulder. "You look extremely handsome, and that little speech you gave was perfect."

"That little speech I gave was written by Bertram," I said.

"Remind me to give him a raise," said mother.

Nobles from all over the kingdom had come to celebrate the young prince becoming an adult. Wealthy merchants of the town were dotted among the crowds, easy to spot because there clothing was made of lower quality materials, their design often a little more experimental and unique than those of the Nobles who had to look their best.

I always envied those in Odette's kingdom, because unique attire for royals and nobles was more common. King William, for example, was decked out in a long navy blue cape with a deep green floral pattern woven with strands of gold.

It was velvet, the same as the rest of his clothing, which hung from him like a garb fit for ... well, for a king. It was much nicer than the plain stuff I would get to wear when I was in his position. Plain with chains.

Although, the reversible jackets customary in my kingdom were pretty interesting.

I scanned the crowd for Odette. I hadn't paid any attention to her because I was so focused on perfectly delivering my speech. She and her father likely went to mingle with the people of our kingdom to make sure everybody got a good impression of them, as if they weren't beloved already.

Everybody in town adored Odette because she was the pinnacle of a perfect young princess, but only when she was in her costume.

I looked for an extravagant gown made of the finest materials, but I couldn't see one. It was all just plain, plain, plain. Rich, but unpatterned. Voluminous, but all in one color.

I finally recognized her by her hair, bigger and brighter than anyone else's. It was the kind of blonde so bright it absorbed the color of nearby light, so it was golden in the glow of the lamps overhead.

I frowned. Her dress wasn't the big, skirt-heavy extravagant ones that most royals and nobles of her kingdom wore. It was far plainer, as was the pattern on it. Simple, pale blue to match my attire, but with golden threading on the bottom that my clothes lacked.

It was quite pretty. I probably should have felt bad about thinking she only looked quite pretty when she was all dressed up, though. That was a change I'd have to make.

This next year would definitely be the year of change. I couldn't let anything like that drunken night happen again. I couldn't be so desperate to prove myself to my best friend that I ended up a blubbering mess, too drunk to function the next day.

I had to be better, and it started today.

"Alright, mother, I'll do as you wish. I'll go mingle now."

Mother clasped her hands together. "Wonderful. Remember, shoulders back, chin up. Make people proud."

Make people proud? It was what I'd been striving to do my whole life. That wasn't going to change now.

Now I had a focus on making people who didn't care about their presentation as much feel, not proud, but at least less irritated with me all the time.

"Odette," I greeted her, just as she turned away from mixing with a group of merchants.

"Prince James," she greeted.

It was hours since we last spoke. We were both whisked away by beauty teams to make us look our best. Well, our second best, anyway. Our Coming-of-Age would have us plucked and preened and styled to sheer perfection, but for now we could look good, but natural. Meaning I still had my eyebrows, while they'd have to be shaped and sculpted when I came of age. Among other things.

"I think it would be wise for us to dance together, given that everybody here knows we're to be married some day. Don't you?"

I proposed it as an observation rather than invitation in case the latter was unappealing.

"It would probably be a good idea, yes. Let's do it."

Odette presented a hand to be taken. I did so lightly, barely grasping it with an index finger and thumb as I led her to the dance floor and assumed the rigid dancing position my tutors over the years drilled into me.

They always told me that when I was actually dancing I'd probably have to relax and be a little more natural. That definitely wasn't going to happen tonight.

Don was dancing with another son of a Lord from our kingdom. Neither of them seemed very good at it. As they spun past us in circles, Don mouthed, "You like her."

It was only the fact that I was holding Odette's hand and waist that stopped me from doing a particularly rude gesture that most princes shouldn't be seen doing at their 18th birthday celebrations. A scowl did the trick, but it only made him smirk.

"What was all that about?" asked Odette.

"Stupid stuff," I said.

We began to move to the music with perfect steps. It seemed we'd both been taught how to dance adequately. Good. And her frame was as rigid as mine for once, which made me smirk almost bigger than Don.

"So. Is this your first big royal duty, then? Other than appearances at the Summer Festival Parade and your father's annual Birthday Ball?"

"It is," said Odette, "and you forgot my introduction into society as a royal young lady when I was 13."

"Oh, right. Yeah, we don't have that here. Princesses are presented at birth and have to look all royal and perfect all the time."

"I'm aware of your customs, yes. I've been reading about them. No wonder you didn't like me when we met—you probably thought I was some sort of wild creature dragged in from the woods."

"I did, come to think of it, yes. But from the town, not the woods."

Our tones were very formal, and yet there was something to them that was nicer, softer, than usual. It didn't feel like we were trying to one up each other or irritate each other much for once.

"Well, royal duties suit you. That's a very nice dress. Not as extravagant as I imagined, though."

"Yeah, the beauty team they gave me tried to put these big fluffy ball gowns with big ruffles and stuff, but I kicked up and threatened to climb out the window and down the rose trellis. They really shouldn't have made me get ready in a room with one of those outside."

Oh, how I resisted the urge not to grin. That story seemed very Odette to me, even though I didn't know her that well, even after all this time.

"That response seems to have worked," I said.

"Yes. I might use it on my own 18th, too. And my Coming-of-Age Ball."

This time I did actually crack a smile. I examined her face to see if she thought it odd, but if she did, it didn't show.

"*You* don't look great," said Odette, and this time I laughed. "No offense, but the giant shoulders that are all pointy at the end are kind of weird. And you call that a cape? It barely comes down to your lower back. What's up with that? I haven't gotten to the chapter explaining your weird fashion yet. I've just read the ones stating what you're supposed to wear."

"I dunno. I never had it explained to me. Growing up they just threw the traditional clothes that me, said they were traditional, and I didn't question it. I never question my duties. I just do them because it's what's right."

Her hand in mine grew stiffer. Her face was became expressionless. I was becoming too much like my old self, wasn't I? The one she first met, the one that led her to dislike me and led to us developing this weird stunted and stagnant relationship in the first place.

"I should question things more," I said. "Like ... like this whole marriage thing. Arranged marriages aren't that uncommon across the land mass, and we're lucky we can at least say no if we want to when the time comes. Do you think it would be more normal for them to set me up with someone my own age? I'm standing here are full-grown adult, and I'm looking at you, and you look all grown up, but you're still only 15. And I know, you're almost 16, but it feels like a lot younger. That's kind of weird, right?"

"Oh, extremely weird. It would be weirder if we weren't forced to kind of grow up together, though. You'd be this big scary strange grown man. But I don't see was that. I just see you as big, annoying Prince James."

For the first time tonight, she smiled at me. I let myself smile back.

"Oh well. In two years you'll be an adult too, and I'll be of age, so I suppose it won't seem as significant then."

"No, I guess it won't."

A new song came on. It seemed we both knew the steps to this, too. She was still rigid, holding her position perfectly, though we weren't quite as tense anymore.

"Do you feel any different?" she asked. "You know, as an adult."

"A little." I had to spin her, as everybody else did during the song. Don and his partner stumbled into the pair next to them, making me snort. "Sorry. I mean, yeah. A little. But also, no. I feel like I'm the same person as I was yesterday, which is true. Just because it's been exactly 18 years since I was born now doesn't make me a different person. But now I feel the weight of more responsibility, the weight of the future more heavily, and the need to ... I don't know. Grow up a little."

"You've been grown up since I met you," said Odette. "The only difference between you then and you now is back then, you used to sit on a fake throne to practice kingly duties. Now you sit in on real meetings and have a real throne to sit on as the adult prince. You just need to ... I don't know. Loosen—"

"Loosen up a little? Yeah, you know how well that went when I tried. But I don't know, maybe you're right. Maybe I was an adult in a child's body but with a childish view of that adulthood. One that I've never really grown out of. Like, I still have a grudge against the tutor who told me my spelling of a word was wrong when I was nine. It wasn't wrong. There are two ways to spell that word, and the one they used is just slightly more common in this kingdom. The one I used is in letters and books from other ones, though. Two years ago, I saw that teacher working with Don's younger brother and I gave them the finger."

"The middle one?"

"Yeah. It's a weird gesture, isn't it? It actually stems from archery—people would wave their middle finger to show it hadn't been blown off or something and it became a universal gesture for a swearword I won't utter."

Odette grinned, almost making me stop our dance in surprise.

"Interesting," she said. "The one time I see you displaying an interest in something that isn't just your training or being a prince, and you won't even say the word associated with the gesture. Oh well." She composed herself again. "So you don't automatically feel more mature?"

"No. No, if anything, I feel more immature. I'm going to work on that. Work on … being less stubborn and set in my childish ways. Maybe by the time I'm of age and can step into an official, full royal role, I'll be somewhat tolerable to people like you."

She rolled her eyes. "Sure."

I found myself smiling, and for the second time in recent weeks, I wondered if I was starting to like it when she did that.

I spun Odette again. This time at the end of the turn, my limbs were slightly less rigid, more fluid like the other dancers.

"Listen," I said, suddenly feeling a weird about how relaxed we'd both become, "do you want to get out of here? Because no offense to the orchestra, but this music is really boring. Plus, I'm kinda sick of everybody staring at us. I know it's going to happen more and more in the future, and it's kind of what they're trained to do from birth, but I need a break."

It was mostly a break from my weirdly muddled thoughts after our little conversation, and when Odette nodded I was filled with relief.

Glancing over my shoulder to ensure mother and the king were sufficiently busy, I dropped Odette's waist and hand. I gestured for her to follow me as we made a beeline for the door.

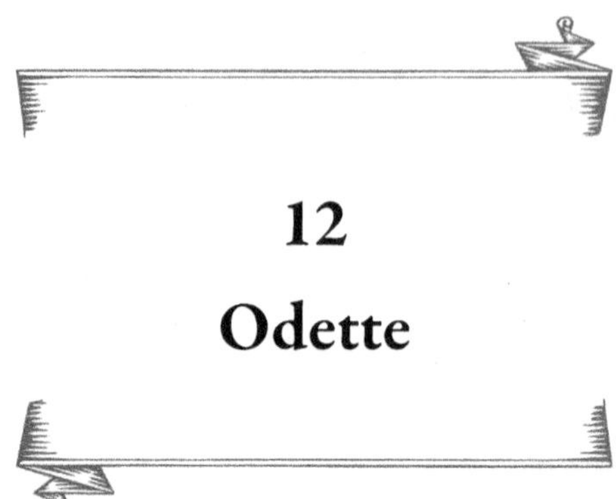

12

Odette

"There's only one place nobody will be looking. Come on. Let's see if there's ice cream in the freezer or something."

I followed James through a part of the castle I'd never been before. There were lots of side corridors and hallways leading from the ballroom. The room he led me to was almost directly below it, a chilly kitchen with a couple of high stools at the counter, much like the kitchen back home but without the chaos.

I hopped onto a stool as James went towards the ice box, grinned, and went to get two bowls.

"So, tell me, Odette" said James, "why is it that you hate dresses and duty so much?"

"After all these years, he finally asks."

"But will you answer?"

"Well, I don't know." I shrugged. "My parents never seemed to like them. So I see them more as an obligation rather than something enjoyable."

Ice cream dished up, James slid a bowl over to me and took a seat opposite.

"Obligations can be enjoyable. For example, tonight is okay. I didn't want a party, but it's turned out alright, hasn't it?"

"I guess," I muttered. "But I bet you didn't want to be with me tonight. So it could be better."

His face betrayed nothing as he said, "No, it's okay. Spending it with you."

Did he mean it, or was he just saying it in an attempt to seem more mature?

We turned our attention to the ice cream. It was that soft stuff, the best kind. It was the one mother always got when we went out. I missed her. If she were still around, I'd have spent this night with her.

"I'm sorry, by the way."

For a minute I thought he was talking about my mother before I got out of my head.

"For what?"

"How I've been over the years. I mean, I guess it made sense at first. We were really different as kids. And then that one summer, do you remember the one where you knocked the treehouse down? Mother had said something that freaked me out, but it was no excuse to shut you out like that. I'm sorry for being so ... cold. Distant."

The sincerity in his voice told me he was being truthful. James struck me as the type of person who wouldn't say something like that unless he really, really meant it.

"It's okay. We weren't just different then. We're still different. We have different values. You're the Perfect Prince ..." Oh no, I couldn't say it, but I'd grinned now so I had to. "And I've got a personality."

The gasp he gave was possibly the biggest emotion I'd ever seen him display sober. He put his hand on his chest and threw his head back, shook it, and feigned an expression of utmost offense.

"How dare you," he said, yet he had a hint of a smile as he returned to a neutral position and began playing with his ice cream.

His eyes were distant, glassy, like he wasn't seeing was in front of him. I looked away, not wanting him to catch me staring.

"I just don't want to be like my father." I looked up. He was staring right at me. "The Drunken King. He was a mess. He didn't care about any of his duties. He let the kingdom down. He drank away our money and much of our respect. Gambled away the rest. Mother says he was ill towards the end, in his head. He never wanted to be king. It got to him. I don't want to let the kingdom down the way he did."

The Drunken King. He said it like it was a fact I already knew.

"You remember," I whispered. "You remember the things you told me that night."

James was still just playing with is ice cream.

"Yeah. But it was easier to pretend I didn't. I don't want to talk about it. Everything I said that night, it was mostly nonsense. Stupid stuff."

So maybe the fact that he liked me a little bit was nonsense too. I supposed right now it didn't matter, because no matter how we felt about each other, we were sharing a moment of pleasantness.

We were silent more than we spoke. I began playing with my ice cream just as he stopped.

"When you're an adult, will you put an end to the summer visits?"

This question took me by surprise. "Coming here is my royal duty," I stated flatly.

"Right. Good for a future marriage, if it happens. That's your royal duty."

"Exactly. And I may not care for royal duties, but I complete them anyway. At least, I have so far."

He pushed his bowl away at last. "I can understand that," he said. "I mean, look at me. I do everything for my kingdom. Everything to be a good ling in the future."

"I do everything to please my father, and my mother when she was alive. And they dropped everything and devoted everything to keep our kingdom running."

James toyed with his sleeve; he pulled so much he got a thread loose and twirled it between his fingers. My hands rested on my lap, my fingers wanting to pick at the nails of the opposite hand just for something to do. I stared at his bowed head.

"You know, you can still complete your royal duties even if you stop coming here when you don't have to anymore." James looked up from his sleeve to address me. "You could stop the visits in two years' time. We could go two years without seeing each other. Then we can get married for the good of the kingdom, live in separate wings of the castle, and do all our duties separately. We'd please our parents, and it would ensure all these years of spending summers together didn't go to waste."

Marriage. It was such a silly thing. It was four years away, which was forever, but then again four years *ago* didn't seem all that long.

Time had a funny way of doing that. Flying when you were living it but seeming an eternity long when it was yet to come.

I wondered if it was normal for other people to have to worry about their marriage years in advance. It didn't seem like it. But then, maybe I was just over-thinking it because I'd never wanted to get married.

"I suppose once it's legally binding, our part is done," I mumbled. If I wasn't going to marry anyone else, I might as well marry him. "And I really don't know if I want to keep coming. If I ever stopped I know I'd miss the Queen. I'd miss your staff. And Bertram, he's wonderful."

"Not me?"

There was something in his eyes, something like hope. I couldn't have been reading him right. But, just in case, I said, "Well, if there are more nights like tonight over the next few years, maybe I'll warm up to you, And if the time comes that I decide to stop coming, I might miss you, too. Maybe."

Another long pause. I was growing tired of them.

"I'd like that," he said.

"You would?"

He nodded. "I'm tired, Odette. I'm tired of being so stiff all the time. Tired of not understanding how I feel. I just want to start over so maybe we can be friends. We'll probably never be good friends, but we can at least be ... friendly friends."

Friendly friends. I rolled my eyes.

"I'm willing to try," I said. I held up my hand, in the exact position I always had to when I arrived and he had to kiss it in greeting. I turned it. He laughed, took it, and shook it.

"Alright," said James. He hopped off the stool, fixed his clothing, and sighed. "We should get back. Shall we go?"

I nodded. After waiting by the door while he washed dishes—something I really didn't expect him to do—I followed him back to the ballroom and hoped we could both keep our promises over the next two summers.

13

James

Why was I so nervous?

All year I'd been leading knightly marches, learning protocols for the things I would do when I was of age, and practicing what would be like to meet other royals when I was of age as the prince, and later, the king.

The duties extended to the summer, too, of course; last year was the first time I found the Summer Festival genuinely fun, sitting side-by-side in a carriage with Odette wearing that silly flower hat and doing the stupid royal wave that we made fun of when nobody was looking.

Oh, and last year was the first time I ever found the royal wave stupid, too.

This year, the Summer Festival would come two days after Odette's 18th birthday, which was only three weeks after my Coming-of-Age Ball.

I couldn't tell if it was the fact that she would finally be an adult soon, or if it was something else, but even in her plain clothes that were often dirty around the ankles, she had a beauty about her that struck me hard. Had she always looked like that? Or was I just noticing it now?

Either way, it made me uncomfortable. So, therefore, I tried not to look at her too often, because despite getting on relatively well from the night of my 18th birthday and on, we still weren't *there*.

No. No, we absolutely were not *there*, and despite Don's constant comments, I did not *like her*.

That would be absurd.

We were more like two friends who'd known each other a few months instead of a few years, and even now we still had our bad days. Old habits.

We weren't ... close. And we weren't yet comfortable.

Although, Odette *was* comfortable enough to tease me about my attempt at letting my hair curl into its natural state for my Coming-of-Age Ball. It irritated me at first, but now it made me laugh because she was right about me looking like an idiot.

"So, what are you doing for your private Coming-of-Age celebration?" asked Odette, sitting across from me at dinner by ourselves.

Mother was busy having many of father's old duties—currently handled by Lord Paxton—over to me. Odette's father was visiting home, helping organize her 18th Birthday Ball coming up in early August. I was nervous, but if it went as well as my 18th and my Coming-of-Age Ball, it would be fine.

We didn't sneak away during my Coming-of-Age Ball like we did at my 18th, but we did spend an awful lot of it standing side-by-side and watching Don attempt to navigate his two left feet, watching the new trumpet player in the orchestra attempts to read the sheet music that was too high for him, and trying to decide whether certain ladies I'd never seen before were hired dates for single and divorced Lords. We concluded there were more hired dates than genuine ones.

"How do you know about my private Coming-of-Age celebration?" I asked.

"It's tradition. I read all about it a couple of summers ago. You're lucky you get a private one. In my kingdom, we just get the ball."

"I'm going out with Don tonight. Also, I think I'm winning this game."

Over the course of the year, Odette had learned a new skill that irritated me to no end. I toyed with the bishop on my chessboard, wondering if I ought to move it.

No moves seemed right, but then again, I was still learning and my "winning" comment was all talk. *She* didn't know I was still learning, but my incompetence so far was probably a giveaway. Plus, I was likely a bad liar.

"Going out with Don? I always knew you two kids would get together," said Odette.

It took me a minute. I laughed. "Yeah. The whole kingdom's been talking about it for years. He's the one I'm supposed to marry, not you."

"It would probably be easier on you to marry him."

"You know what? You're probably right. Best friends to lovers. If only I liked men. Well, who knows? I might. I've never considered it." I gazed at her as she smiled. "I've never considered liking women, either."

She raised her eyebrows. "Well, you should probably start considering it soon. We're getting married in two years."

"Well, not considering it is your fault. Knowing I was going to end up with you anyway, I never gave any of it a second thought."

Although, thinking about woman in *that* way was what tonight was all about. Not that I'd tell her that.

"What are you two doing?" said Odette, becoming serious again.

"We're going out for drinks."

"Are you sure that's wise? Check."

If there was ever a moment to swear it would be now, but I muttered, "Fiddlesticks." I returned to my normal volume. "And yes, it is wise. Two drinks, then I'll switch to non-alcoholic cider. I can't be drunk. He's taking me somewhere after that he's been going since he was 18, somewhere his father goes a lot. I'm going to ... learn a thing or two. He's been trying to get me to go for two years, so I thought I owed it to him."

"You thought *you* owed *him* on *your* private Coming-of-Age celebration?"

"Well, he's put up with a lot over the years, so yeah."

She gave me this sweet little smile, but her eyes weren't pleased. Maybe she wanted an invitation. Private Coming-of-Age celebrations usually took place with all of the royal's friends, which we were, of course.

But she couldn't come tonight. I'd burst into flames if she so much as knew a *hint* of what Don had planned for me after the drinks.

Was it weird to organize for your best friend to go watch people in a whore house getting it on for their birthday? Maybe, but he said it was how he learned what to do before his first time with his last girlfriend and his current boyfriend, so...

"And," I said quickly, "I ... think part of my private celebration is having a second private celebration. But I don't know what that'll be yet. Maybe you and I could do something? Like a joint private celebration of my Coming-of-Age and your 18th. We could do it after your ball, since you won't be getting a private Coming-of-Age celebration in two years. It'll make up for last summer, too, when Don forgot to invite you to the celebration for my 19th."

Don was still getting used to the fact that Odette and I were trying to be friendly now. She hadn't seemed upset when Don set up a jousting tournament for me that he and I would be partaking in alongside some other people he knew who were into it. He hadn't even thought to invite Odette to *watch*, and forgetting her wasn't something I was eager to repeat.

Despite not showing her hurt outwardly, her eyes were duller for the rest of the summer. And, worst of all, she may have been planning something for me, too. I overheard her talking to Bertram about a cake, but it never showed up once I returned from the tournament, eager to share stories of it.

Ooh, that was some guilt I didn't like reliving. I supposed I was at fault there, too—I hadn't thought to invite Odette either.

"I'd like that," said Odette, dragging me back to the present, and my offer that would hopefully make up for last summer. "You're still in check, by the way."

I sighed. "I fold."

"You can't fold. It isn't poker."

"I don't care. As I'm of age now, I can legally approve and make up new laws. So the law now states that chess players can now fold if they wish. But ... they have to be royals. Oh, and of age. So next time I beat you, or I'm about to beat you, you can't fold. Feel free to in two years, though."

"Next time you beat me?" Odette folded her arms. "You mean the *first* time you beat me. Which, at this rate, I think will take two years to happen."

I really liked her little comebacks like that. Though I had to feign offense, which she rolled her eyes at.

"Speaking of being of age," said Odette, "what's it like? I know it hasn't been long, but I've hardly seen you."

"Yeah, I know. There are lots of procedures to learn. I'm booked solid for the next two years, going off on all these royal appearances that I wouldn't usually have to go on with mother. Kingdoms all over the land mass. And I get to knight someone for the first time next week. It's usually the king or oldest male monarch's job to knight male knights, and the Queen's or oldest female monarch's job tonight female knights in our kingdom, and if they're not male or female then they can choose who they're knighted by—but you already knew all that."

"Yes. And I already knew you'd be booked solid for years, visiting other kingdoms. Here, when a new royal comes of age, they essentially do a royal tour, don't they? Visiting all the allies. We don't have that in my kingdom. We send out letters instead."

"Oh? Would you rather travel?"

"Well, maybe. But if I'm going to travel, I'd like to go out on the ocean and go somewhere more exciting than another kingdom here. Although, the kingdom of the West Coast does seem exciting. And some of those kingdoms with magic—"

I threw up my hands. "Oh no. I'm not talking about magic. Mother hates it. Magical creatures, magical spells, magic books. And I don't want to fight, so let's just avoid the topic."

Odette nodded. "Fair enough."

"Why do you ask, by the way?"

"What?"

"About what it's like being of age. You sounded genuinely curious. I would've thought it would be something you're dreading."

"Oh, I am. Hell, I'm dreading turning 18. Because it means I have start to training properly for the things I'll be doing when I'm Queen. I know it's not the same. I know you're going through a lot more. But it's a big change."

Hell. It was almost a swear. Even now, on the cusp of adulthood, she didn't seem like any royal I'd ever met; they would never swear. That used to bother me, but now it fascinated me. She was so solidly Odette, so much herself no matter what. I can tell if I admired that was envious.

"You'll make a good Queen," I stated. "Even when you don't want to do something, you step up. Like coming here every summer. And like that obnoxiously gigantic dress you wore to my Coming-of-Age Ball—did they not put you in the room with the rose trellis under the window this time?"

"No, they did. But they locked the window and hid the key."

I couldn't tell if it was a joke, but I laughed all the same.

It felt like there was a natural lull in the conversation, and we fell silent again but didn't start another game. She toyed with one of her knights, twirling it around and around in different directions. I watched those fingers work, kind of afraid to look at her face in case it betrayed her thoughts.

There was one on my mind that weighed on it for all of last summer, and returned now with more force than ever.

'So, have you made up your mind?"

"What?"

"About whether or not you're going to leave and stop the visits once you're an adult."

"Oh. Oh, I ..." I looked in her eyes only to find they darted downward. "I don't know yet. Last summer wasn't bad. I mean, I enjoyed that walk we took. And our horse riding trips. Our conversations were about nonsense, but they were okay. I realized you're easy to talk to, even if just about stupid stuff."

"Listen, the best dressed Lord in the kingdom and the ugliest tree in the garden are perfectly reasonable and exciting topics of conversation!" I said, folding my arms to try and make her laugh, but every time I attempted it, it didn't seem to work. I just got that classic eye roll. Maybe that was how she expressed amusement. I liked to think so.

"If you say so, Your Royal Highness," she said. "Anyway ..." She sighed. "So, I haven't decided yet. Because there are so many other things I could be doing during the summer. The town around my castle has all kinds of festivals, and I have tons of ideas for different things I want to do not just for the town, but the kingdom, and yours. I have plans to make. And I have things I want to see and places I want to go, and I could spend summers doing that.

"I have books I want to read, people I want to meet. I'd like to make friends of my own, really start ... I don't know. Living. It will be hard in between my new duties, and fitting in visits here will only make it harder. But if there's something here that's worth my while staying for, then I could try to balance all three."

"And what would make it worth your while?"

She finally looked at me, instead of looking around the room and just in vague directions as she spoke. She opened her mouth to talk again, but she couldn't do it while our gaze was locked.

"I think we're friends now. I mean, you're still the most annoying person I've ever met, but I think we're ... we're getting somewhere. We're like friends in a village school house who are only friends because they're in forced proximity, but that feels like a foundation for something. And if I feel like it's worth erecting something on top of that foundation, then I'll keep coming. But if by the end of the summer it feels like a lost cause, then I'll see you in two years and see where it goes."

Now she looked at me, and there were so many things in that gaze that I couldn't interpret. Maybe what I saw in it was wishful thinking, but she looked apologetic. Nervous. Determined. Maybe a touch sad.

"I know one thing for sure," I said, "you seem to have this more well thought out than me, so I won't request to stop the visits. I'm going to leave it all up to you."

Odette smiled. "Oh, James. I never thought for a second you'd be the one to stop the visits. Because in your kingdom, a young prince can stop visits with his potential intended when he turns 13, and I'm sure that's something your mother would have told you at that age. I think it's worth something that you've kept trying all these years, and if you didn't stop our visits then, you're certainly not going to do it now."

14

Odette

"**D**ammit, dammit, dammit!"

His every exclamation made me laugh harder. Losing at poker was the closest James ever came to swearing, and yet still his expulsions of irritation were so tame.

"Poor Prince," I sighed, "foiled again. I swear, you'd think you'd learn to fold. You're really not very good at this, are you?"

"I am," said James, through gritted teeth. "I always fold if I even *suspect* my hand might be slightly weaker than yours. I'm so tired of losing. I just want to win *one* time, but every time I think I'm going to, *you* fold. It's ridiculous. How many years have we been playing this game?"

"Let me think," I said, tilting my head and chewing my lip. "How many years have I been finding this room stupid? I swear, I'm tired of trying not to bump into things on my way to the card table, and I'm tired of not being able to play at night. The lighting in this corner—"

"You made your point very clear when you wrote out instructions for me to rearrange it when you were 13," said James. "Quite frankly, I don't care. Not being able to come in here at night just means I'm not able to *lose* at night."

I giggled. He raised his eyebrows, like he'd never heard me do that before. I supposed I *didn't* do it around him often; he never gave me reason to.

"Look," I said.

Did I really want to give up my secret? Oh, I'd kept it for the better part of a decade. But seeing his poor, defeated little face made it harder and harder to keep mine straight.

I got satisfaction in keeping things from him, exchanging looks with Donald and wondering if Donald was going to tell. Although Don and I never got along, it seemed he was on my side and at least one regard.

Though in his case it was probably because he kept winning candy and coins from James.

James and I only ever played for ego, though. So I'd lose nothing I'd miss by finally giving in.

"Look what?"

"Can I let you in on a secret?" I placed my cards down, trying not to laugh at the exasperation on his face as he leaned across the table.

"Please do."

"You have a tell."

The cards in James's hands bent as his hands balled into fists.

"I have a *what*?"

I laughed again, only making his eyes narrow and his teeth grit harder.

"When you have a good hand, you lick your lower lip. We have a *really* good hand, you lick your lower lip and raise your eyebrows a fraction. When you have a bad hand, even when you're bluffing, you raise your eyebrows and bite your lip just slightly, grazing it with your top teeth. You've always done it. I've never lost satisfaction in trying to figure out when you'd notice."

James dropped the cards and slammed his palm on the table. "Does Don know about this?"

"Yeah, actually. Your best friend isn't as loyal to you as you thought. *Everyone* knows. Remember the one time your mother came in here? How do you think she got you to host the Funds for Our Elders campaign when Lord Wesley dropped out? It's because she knew about the tell. And Bertram and I talk about it every time you storm out of here and I walk out grinning. I wouldn't be surprised if there's a betting pool trying to figure out when you're going to realize you've got it. None of us so far have ever been tempted to break and tell you."

"I hate everyone in this damn castle," James grumbled, but after a moment, he seemed to come to his senses and shake out of it. "So, why tell me now?"

I shrugged. "It felt like time. It's felt like it would be funny to see your reaction rather than let it continue and see you lose. And it was really worth it.

Now I get to see you try to figure out how to not do your tells, and that's going to be even better."

James's cheek twitched. The internal battle of rage and perhaps a desire to act smug and pretend he knew seem to wage within him, and I was prepared for whatever came out. I was always prepared for what I came out of him—James was the most predictable person I'd ever met.

He got to his feet, paused a moment, and with one great sweep, almost everything on the table flew onto the floor, or flew into the air and landed somewhere else in the room.

"From now on, we play chess," he stated. "You can't have a tell with chess."

"No, but you can show your shortcomings in logic, strategy, and forward thinking."

"Oh, bite me, Princess," James muttered, probably thinking I wouldn't hear him as he stomped almost louder than he spoke on his way to get the chessboard.

I went easy on him during our first game. Maybe I felt bad for him, or maybe I just thought it would be funny when he lost after doing better than usual. *He* didn't need to know that I choreographed the entire thing, ensuring we reached a stalemate.

"Told you I was getting better at this," he grinned. "I may not be able to beat you yet, little princess, but I can at least match your skills."

My response was to obliterate him within two moves in the next game, leading him to hiss under his breath and stomp around for several minutes, evaluating other games we could play, before he sat down again.

"I need some air," said James.

"You need some better game skills," I retorted.

"I'm going out," he said. He seized his little princely jacket off the back of the chair and shrugged it on upside down, let out a roar, then put it on the right way up.

My mirth irritated him further, but his anger melted away once he got his jacket on right.

"Thank you, by the way," he said.

"For what?"

"Telling me about the tell," he said. "But I *will* get you back for it eventually."

"I look forward to it."

And I meant it, too.

Yet several days passed, and there was no sign of his revenge. We didn't spend much time in the game room, instead choosing to spend our days doing our own activity side-by-side.

When I mentioned wanting to read, he took me into a little back section of the library and showed me all these dusty volumes. He pulled scrolls from shelves willy-nilly and tore one, making me wince as he hastily shoved it back on the shelf and tried to make it look like nobody had touched it, though his finger prints were clear in the dust.

He did paperwork and studied dutiful things while I read and watched him grit his teeth every time something in the paperwork confused him, trying not to laugh at him all the while.

The next day, he brought me down to his stables and introduced me to the blacksmith while he set up a little animatronic dummy thing nearby that he'd imported from another kingdom. He used it to practice dueling with swords.

He was good, but the strange animatronic scarecrow thing was strangely skilled for an object.

It seemed after all this time he was finally paying attention to doing things I liked rather than just having me tag along with him or do something aimless.

I began to really like our days spent doing our own thing side-by-side. Essentially, it was good practice for our future.

I tried out pottery while he attempted it for five minutes, swiftly quit, and instead turned to flicking through printed volumes to pick out traditional outfits he approved for future ceremonies and duties.

He tried out cooking and found himself good at it while I played solitaire, read between games, and picked out cheeses to bring to the mice in the bushes who only came out at night.

It was like for the first time he was actually listening to me, responding to what I liked and what I didn't, because he never took me cooking again but frequently brought me back to make pottery in the basement.

He'd often sit by my side as I learned to make horseshoes, getting my hands dirty rather than observing for the first time in my life. And when the potter helped me make my first vase, James boasted my skills to Queen Euberta.

Several times he even brushed Don off for minor things, because he seemed to favor spending time with *me*. I'd *never* had a friend who chose me over someone else. My heart swelled with appreciation I'd never dare share.

"I'm glad to see you're getting along," said father, when I showed up to dinner one day holding a big volume about amphibians that James picked out for me after he'd heard I'd stopped to talk to a frog during one of my nightly walks with my father. "It's easier, isn't it?"

"Much," I said. "Although I should just remind you that it was never me that was the problem. He was the unpleasant one and I just tagged along. And he made no effort to change, so I made no effort to reach out to him. Now that he's changing, he's actually nice. Maybe one day I'll wake up and find I miss him when I'm doing something and he's not in the corner doing something else."

Father laughed. "Here's hoping."

Queen Euberta joined us at the table. James was still washing up from his second attempt at pottery, which he still detested. I theorized he was trying to find something he liked doing other than all the royal stuff.

It was about time James branched out, and perhaps I ought to tell him I was impressed he was trying.

"Good evening," said the Queen, beaming.

Bertram walked in shortly behind the queen and addressed my father at once.

"King Richard—I've sent Barnus to talk to Cleo as you asked. If you're ready, you could be on a boat after dinner."

"Boat?" I asked father.

Father put down his utensils.

"Oh, yes. Sorry to say, but I'm going to be gone for a few days, Odette."

My heart sank. "You said you wouldn't be going away again this summer."

"I know, I know," said father, "But I just want to go check on how things are going at home one last time before your birthday."

Father exchanged a look with the queen, whose eyes twinkled.

"I know you're going to love it," said father. "And I know, I know, you hate balls, but trust me, this one will be worth attending. Consider it an apology for years of attending ones you don't like and for the one in thwo years where you have to be tortured beforehand."

Father unconsciously rubbed underneath his eyebrow. I grinned. James had been doing that occasionally, too, and although I'd have to go through the beautification process in a few years, it still amused me to see others going through it now.

"It's much worse for those who choose to present themselves as feminine," said Queen Euberta, shuddering. "My sister was pledged to a queen in another kingdom when she came of age, and she didn't have to do any of that stuff because she preferred to wear masculine clothes. Short hair and the likes. She got the typical man's treatment. But girls like us? Oh, we're not so lucky."

I look towards father. "Is it too late to start dressing like you?"

Father laughed. "It's never too late, but considering you cried when you had a short haircut when you were four, I don't think you'd like it. But you *will* like the ball. Trust me."

"I do." I sighed. "So does that mean you won't be here for our nightly walk tonight?"

"I'm afraid so," said father.

"What's going on?" asked James, arriving with clean hands at last.

"King Richard will be going away for a couple of days, so the two of you will only have one monarch and myself to drive insane with your youthful antics," said Bertram, making Queen Euberta chuckle. "I'm joking, of course."

"Indeed," said father. "Honestly, your'e two of the most well-behaved royals there are."

"Well, apart from the nights you sneak out and think your mother doesn't know about it, James," said Bertram.

Sneaking out? I glanced at James, who went bright red.

"It's Don's fault," he muttered.

"Shame," said Queen Euberta. "Because every real prince starts to rebel at some point, and I was hoping you'd finally reached that stage. Really, I've been waiting for one drunken night foray into a house of ... well, there's a young lady present, so I'm not going to finish that sentence."

She sat up a little straighter, and I hid my face behind my hair. I couldn't fight back the smirk. There may have been a young lady present, but I was a well-read young lady who'd read enough books and overheard enough conversations to know what kind of *house of* ... she meant.

"Yet there's been nothing so far," the queen continued. "Not even a tipsy evening where you had one glass of wine too many with dinner!"

I glanced at James, trying not to smile. Although his one drunken night had been caused by his best friend, I was sure if Queen Euberta knew about it she'd still count it as an act of rebellion.

"So, when are you leaving, King Richard?" asked James, overtly turning away from his mother.

"Right after dinner," said father, "so I'll be there by morning. I prefer to travel at night. It feels much more productive to sleep rather than lose a whole day on a ship."

An hour later, I waved father off at the castle gate. Queen Euberta accompanied me, but James stayed inside. When we turned away to head back towards the castle, she put a hand on my shoulder.

"How about a spot of after-dinner tea?" she asked. "It won't make up for your usual night-time walk with your father, and I know how much you love those, but it's better than nothing."

As much as I appreciated it, I shook my head.

"I'm okay. I think I'm just going to go to my room and read for a while. I might go out by myself later."

"Whatever you want, dear. Very well."

I didn't expect my father to spend every evening with me, but for the past few years our evening walks had been a touch of home laced throughout the summers away.

This place was so familiar it was like a second home to me, yet still, my *actual* home had memories that I could never replicate anywhere else.

Reading helped, learning fascinating facts that made me view the world with more appreciation, but now the evening felt like it was missing something.

I sighed, flicking through the volume about amphibians, wishing I was outside instead. I just didn't see the point in going alone, and the mice didn't feel like they'd be chatty enough company tonight.

I was contemplating going to bed early when there was a knock on my door. James was the last person I expected to see when I opened it.

"Hi," he said. "Do you want to go for a walk?"

"Like, outside?"

"No, Odette, I thought we'd go for a walk along the ceilings." He sighed. "Yes, outside. I thought you might be bored stuck inside when you're used to getting out with good company. And I may not be good, but I am company. What do you say?"

It was either go out with James or learn about frogs. The latter seemed a better choice, but still ...

"That would be nice," I said. The frogs could wait.

James gestured for me to follow him, so I did, out into the hall always walking a step behind him and a couple of steps to the side. We didn't talk, but I thought a lot. We were almost halfway to the outside before I asked, "Am I not interrupting your evening??"

"Oh, please," said James. "Most nights I just listen to music and throw balled up paper into a waste basket as a kind of sport. Or I just look out the window. Sometimes I wonder around the castle, or I go out with Don. You're not interrupting anything important."

"Oh. Well, okay." We fell silent again. We'd gone on walks before, long ones at that, and after our conversation earlier I felt much more comfortable with him than I had in years.

Still, it just felt weird to be with anyone other than my father at this time of day.

It was late enough for the sun to be growing lower in the sky, and the castle was at its quietest point. It felt like another world on this late summer eve, the typically warm air now colder with the breeze that felt better against my skin than the daytime sun.

"So, you look out the window?" I asked.

"Yeah, sometimes," said James. My feet found the familiar path I usually went with my father, one James was also going down without being directed. "I sometimes look at the stars and think of the stories my mother used to tell me when I was small. About the shapes and everything. About their connections and meanings. Then I get bored, sometimes I look down at the garden, watching the wildlife. More often than not you and your father are there, but I always lose sight of you when you disappear behind the arch out of the training grounds."

I knew he didn't mean it that way, but my skin tingled slightly at the thought that he'd been watching me. Maybe all summer, maybe for several in a row.

"How come you never called out and said hello?" I asked.

"I never wanted to interrupt. You always look your happiest when you're with someone who's not me."

The disappointment in his tone hurt slightly, although I probably imagined it. There was no way he'd be disappointed by my enjoyment of spending time with others but not him.

"Well, you could've said hello. Or you could've come and join us. After all, it's your castle."

"It's my mother's castle. But like I said, I didn't want to interrupt. Anyway, fireflies kinda freak me out. I don't like any big ... flying ... *thing*."

One of the bushes we passed was dotted with fireflies as we spoke. He gave them a glance that showed me the he was more fearful than unappreciative of their beauty.

"Oh, please," I scoffed. "What's a little firefly going to do to a big, gallant prince like you? Glow you to death?"

"You don't know," said James. "Maybe. Plus, other stuff lurks in the bushes. There are wolves in the forest, and big, giant rats around, too."

"The rats won't hurt you," I replied. "They don't care about you at all. *I* think they're cute."

"*I* think *you're* insane."

"Yeah, but you always have."

He grinned, and he didn't see as I did the same in response. I let it fall as his face fell into a more neutral one, looking out ahead. I wondered perhaps when we passed the training grounds if he'd want to skirt over there instead as it was a more familiar place for him to wander. But no, he continued on my usual path, letting me admire all the flowers that I'd come to know the names and bloom cycles of over the summer.

"You're not insane," said James eventually, as if we'd just finished talking about it. "I mean, you scare me, but other people might find your affection for wild animals and rodents and ... big ugly glowing bugs ... charming. Maybe they'd call you a Princess for the ... I'm not smart enough to know a word for animals or creatures that starts with P. 'Puny creatures' sounds kind of rude." He paused, shaking his head.

"What are you talking about?"

"You know, it's the kind of thing you read about in books describing great royals of the past. Some are known for doing great in battle or growing their kingdoms or getting them out of poverty. Others are just known because they used to save birds from stray cats or something. And they get nicknames for it. 'King of Klashes,' but spelled with a 'K' instead of a 'C.' 'Prince for the Poor.' 'Princess Beatrice of the Birds' and all that. That's the one who saved the birds from stray cats." When I looked at him with surprise, he shrugged and said, "See, I read. Sometimes."

"I did that when I was a kid," said Odette. "The cat thing. Well, it wasn't from a stray. It was a cat I had when I was four. I used to save field mice and rats and other things from it."

"See, what did I say?" James laughed. "It's stuff like *that* that makes you beloved by all, trust me. You'll be the perfect princess or the beloved queen and I'll just be the king who's there by your side who nobody really cares about."

"Oh, I'm sure people will care about you. Or they'll at *least* talk about you. You could be the ... the King of Clunky Haircuts. Or ... the King Who Cooked One Time or the King Who ... Tolerates the Insane Queen Who Saves Rodents From Cats and Talks to Frogs."

He laughed.

It was a nice image, the pair of us, a strange duo who hadn't always gotten along but who'd learned to tolerate each other's quirks.

I once hated those quirks, the rigid and dull ones where he seemed to have no personality other than caring about his royal duties and what not, but it was now ... acceptable to me. Almost amusing. Plus, understanding where it came from made me see it differently.

"Well, maybe I'll start talking to frogs, too," said James. "And they'll call me the Frog Prince." He frowned. "Actually, no, I think there's a princess who married a guy who was turned into a frog. So scratch that."

"There was," I said, "but he was cursed. A human cursed and turned into a frog. It's weirdly common throughout history. Sometimes they're made into talking frogs, or frogs who are people by day and frogs by night. It never happens in kingdoms like ours, though. It's always ones with magic."

"Magic," James repeated distastefully. "If I didn't know it existed, I wouldn't believe in it."

"No?"

"No. It just seems really far-fetched. People with powers and people who can turn into animals ... come on. Don't you think that sounds ridiculous?"

I shrugged. We'd come to the large rock that father and I often sat on. It was flanked by bushes covered in fireflies.

I sat. James hesitated before taking a seat next to me. It was quite a narrrow rock, so we were closer than we'd ever been apart from when we danced at all those balls.

I'd usually have the urge to move away, but I was surprisingly comfortable.

"Magic is by no means far-fetched," I stated.

"Oh yeah? What makes you think so?"

"Let's think," I said. "Well, scientists on the West Coast have invented things that let them look at things in the sky that aren't stars, but are what they believe are whole other worlds like ours. Archaeologists in my kingdom dug up bones of creatures that inspired a whole new branch of science called palaeontology, and they believe millions of years ago there were giant reptile creatures that lived on the planet before we did.

"There's a big round thing in the sky that looks like a world like ours but smaller, and if we could fly I have no doubt we could land on it. It has the potential to be full of living things just like us, or totally different from us, because do you see any water on it? No. So different types of creatures would have to evolve on it who don't need water. Maybe they don't even need air to breathe."

I paused, my heart pounding. James stared at me as he never had before. The silence hurt my ears, so I filled it with further rambling.

"And there are even creatures *here* the don't breathe normal air. They breathe air out of water. If we did that, we'd drown. And if we strapped on big fake wings, we couldn't fly, but there are creatures who can soar through the skies, creatures of all shapes and sizes who can do it.

"We cohabit with four-legged creatures with long faces who make funny noises and that we can use for transport. We also cohabit with these slinky, furry little things that catch birds and mice, and these big happy things that are just like smaller wolves with waggy tails.

"A big fiery ball gives us light and heat that's stronger sometimes and weaker other times. When it's weaker, white stuff falls from the sky. Sometimes even when it's strong, the sky screams and sends sparks down and pours water on us.

"All of these things seem normal. Because we think they are. Because we've always lived with them so nobody ever thought to question it.

"To people from a world where none of this occurred, it would seem like magic, or maybe madness. So it's not that far-fetched to imagine there are other impossibilities.

"I mean, if little winged insects were once little wormy ones, how is it impossible to believe a person could turn into an animal? Or if smart people with liquids and solids in little tubes can make explosions and create new metals and things by mixing different substances together and applying forces to them, why is it impossible to think that people could make things simply with power, forces or substances held in their own body instead?"

I went quiet. The silence screamed louder than ever. James was still. staring at me. My heart grew loud in my ears, and my body shook, because I felt silly.

This was the kind of thing I talked about with my father, not with James. It was the kind of thing I read about but didn't discuss. Now I'd shown him I thought about all these weird things, and he was going to laugh at me for thinking they were abnormal or akin to magic.

My friends in childhood always did; they called me Princess *Odd*ette and left me for their other friends who weren't so strange.

"Wow." When James finally spoke, it was a whisper that killed the scream of the silence. "And I thought you were observant when you told me I had tells playing poker."

I laughed, looking down. The pressure left my shoulders, eased in my head.

A slight breeze caught my hair and pushed it into my face. Before I could raise my hand to push it back behind my ear, James had done it for me.

"Thanks," I said.

"You're welcome," he said. "You know, I ... I never thought to question any of that. I never really thought to question anything. Hell, it wasn't until I met you that I realize people could be different to how they are in my kingdom, and it wasn't until I observed you for a few years that I started finding it interesting. I've been living in a little bubble, haven't I?"

I shrugged. "Yeah, but that's okay. Most people do. And they all think everyone else does, too."

My hair blew into my face again, but James caught it before it had the chance to bother me. His gaze was more intense than the silence from earlier, his silence no longer fueling my anxiety.

I could talk to him. He wouldn't leave me if I did.

"Like, you probably think I just look at the mice because I think they're cute or something," I said, wondering if he cared of if he was just being polite, "But no. I like to observe their behaviors, wondering what's going on in their heads. Wondering if they have thoughts or language or a form of intelligence beyond what we've observed.

"And you probably just think I like making stuff and working with my hands when I'm with the blacksmith, but no. I like seeing how this substance bends and melts and can be warped when placed in fire, and it fascinates me how there are things so strong they can be set ablaze until they're glowing red hot, yet if we even get too close to a flame, we could get burned."

Still, he didn't speak. I could risk one more thought, one more before it put such a strain on my head that it would ache.

"I just think there's more to life than doing what's expected of us and doing duties and ... sitting around and waiting for things to happen to us in these perfect little lives we've crafted for ourselves as a society."

I was trembling now. This was something I'd confessed to my father here years ago, stunning him into silence. He blinked a lot, raised his eyebrows, shuffled around and asked me how I got so smart. And then we moved on like we never discussed it, like it was something he never wanted to question.

Any moment now, James would do the same, and I'd be left alone with my thoughts, alone to do whatever I wanted while keeping my reasons to myself.

"You can laugh," I said, thinking it better than silence. "Go on, laugh."

"I'm not laughing," said James.

My eyes hadn't been focused on anything particular. I turned towards him and said, suddenly terrified by the intensity of the look he was still giving me. My throat was dry.

"I think you're incredible," he said. Some life came back into him, the intensity ebbing away. "I mean, really incredible. Maybe I would've noticed it years ago if I'd actually been paying attention. I just ... wow."

He leaned towards me. I still wasn't uncomfortable even though I should have been.

"When we get married, I want you to teach me about all of that," he said. "No. I can't wait until then. I need you to come back here every summer and teach me about all of that. I want to do whatever I can to make it right, to make up for all those years of not paying attention. Because that's—"

He cut off and just laughed. It wasn't the same kind of laugh that my father gave me, amused at my overthinking. It was something else. He was smiling in a way I'd never seen before, not rigid and stiff like Prince James, but possibly the smile of the real person hiding underneath the front he presented to the world.

I quite liked that smile. It made him look ... pretty? Almost? Or at least appealing in some way. A nice. Like someone I wanted to be here with and who wasn't a consolation prize for the evening.

"Yeah, I'll do that," I said quietly. "I'll teach you everything you want me to if you really want me to stay." I still hadn't made up my mind. I knew he wasn't going to end our visits, but still, I couldn't help but wonder if he wanted me to do it instead. "Do you want me to stay? Or would you rather I—"

A rustle in the bushes made me turn my head. The last time those bushes rustled so loudly it was because James was in them, years earlier, stumbling home drunk. Today, a head popped out, grinning.

"James," hissed Donald. "Oh, um, hi, Odette. James, come here. You have to come out with me tonight. The Secret Bar has got this new alcohol that tastes like fruit, and they mix it all up in this little silver thing and it shakes really loudly, and it's the best thing I've ever tasted. And it's Anita's night off. You know, Anita from ... *that* place?"

I looked at James. For the first time in my life, I didn't want him to leave. I'd usually yearn for Don to come and distract him, take him away from me, but not now. Not tonight. Not when he might have been finally telling me if he wanted me here, truly.

James turned between Donald and I, mouth partially open, and I knew he didn't want to be here with me as much as I suddenly favored being in his company.

"It's all right," I said dully. "You can go."

James beamed. "You're the best," he said.

In an instant, what felt like the thick protective bubble surrounding us shattered, and the night became normal again. My flurry of thoughts now floating around us were forced back into my body, and that was that.

"Have fun," I muttered.

James barely looked back at me and gave me the thumbs up behind his back as I stood up and made to go back towards the castle. Donald was talking excitedly as he pulled James through the bush, and it rustled once more a moment after they'd seemingly gone through it, but I didn't care enough to look back.

No matter how much had changed, no matter how many nice little talks we had, there was always going to be something else that James was more interested in than he was in me.

15

James

I didn't think she'd mind. Why would she mind? She never minded!

The pain on her face as I left made me come back, because hurting her was the last thing I wanted to do. After so many years, I had a lot to make up for, and I thought last summer was a great start until that fiasco for my birthday.

This summer was a fresh start, a clean slate to have no bad days, but apparently that wasn't going to happen.

"Come on, James," said Don, as I tried to find Odette's retreating back in the darkness, but she'd already gone. "You still want to come, don't you? I mean, you can invite her if you want—it might be a little tough to explain who Anita is and where you met her, but you could definitely bring her. The Secret Bar would love to have a princess in it."

I shook my head. "She doesn't want to come."

"You always say that. Maybe if you actually asked—"

"Trust me, Don." I turned back towards him, his head poking comically out of the bush. "This time, I *definitely* know she doesn't want to come."

And honestly, after that, I wasn't sure I wanted to go, either.

Was it all in my head? She *had* told me on several occasions that she didn't dislike me. But "didn't dislike" didn't equate to like, did it?

And here I didn't just mean like as in liking me as a person, as someone to be around—clearly it was something more. As in ... *like* like.

She was almost 18. We'd be on level playing ground, just two adults who'd known each other forever. There was nothing stopping her from acknowledging any feelings she had buried deep down under the surface.

Maybe, when I told her I kind of liked her, she took it to mean *that* kind of like. When I said it, I *was* trying to hide the fact that it maybe, kind of, shouldn't have but kind of did, mean ... that.

But now, of course, she thought I didn't care about her in the slightest, always choosing my best friend over her.

"Listen, she'll understand," said Don, throwing an arm over my shoulders as we walked through the town, taking the back alleys.

I needed to take Odette back here someday. From what I heard, if she wanted to go out in her town, she had to go in disguise. That was what she'd been doing when her mother died.

But here, there were a couple of establishments—okay, not ones worthy of taking a princess to on a regular day, but whatever—that were reachable without venturing out into the main area where everybody would stare at somebody cloaked and stare harder at a royal.

Maybe I had to pencil that into the celebration I was planning, my second private celebration for my Coming-of-Age and her private birthday celebration.

Goodness. What did Odette like?

"Do we have one of those *places*?" I asked.

"What?" said Don.

"You know, one of those places. One of those places they store all the things. Old books and stuff."

"You mean a library?"

"No, because there are also paintings. And now bones and things."

"Oh!" said Don. "You mean a museum? Yeah, one opened a couple of months ago. Lord Pearce sponsored it or something. It was when you were away visiting your cousin."

"Museum," I said, "that's it. Okay, good."

The museum would surely require a guard to get to, because I doubted it was a shady establishment on the back side of town, but it was worth it. That was somewhere else I'd have to take Odette. The museum.

And then, I knew of this little place where they kept all kinds of animals and stuff in nice and humane habitats, including bugs like fireflies and other horrifying—um, interesting—creatures. Maybe I'd take her there, too.

A full day of trips, followed by a nice night ... in the game room.

In the *rearranged* game room!

It was the perfect celebration, mixed with it being a hidden apology for years of ups and downs. We'd do it the day after her birthday, the day after the ball. I'd travel home by night to make sure everything was ready by that morning. Perfect.

"I wasn't interrupting anything, was I?" asked Don. "You and Odette, I mean. I didn't expect to see you both out there. You looked like you were sitting … really close together. And having some kind of conversation. I mean, I guess that's what people do, isn't it? But … oh, you know what I mean."

For once, his rambling didn't make me laugh.

"We were having an interesting chat," I said. "Actually, an eye-opening one. One that should have never ended. But it's too late now, and I'll make it up to her. Hey, do they have pens and paper at the bar? I want to make a list so I don't forget."

Don pulled his arm from around me so he could take a step to the side and give me a *look*.

"You're weird," said Don, and I laughed. "You're not acting like yourself. Where's the, 'one drink, one conversation, and then we need to get off home' prince from last week? You know, good old Mr. 'okay, I'll stay late, but you have to bring me coffee in the morning because I need to be up early to sign some papers for the royal decree of … something stupid.'"

I rolled my eyes. "I don't sound like that."

"Oh, and of course, there's Mr. 'don't keep me out too late, because mother is going to be away at breakfast with King Richard, so it will just be me and Odette. I don't want her to think I'd ever be late to something, or that I'm ditching her. But then again, maybe I should be late, fashionably late, so she doesn't think I'm so uptight and obsessed with scheduling like a lot of royals are, and like I actually am, but—'"

"Oh, shut up," I scoffed. "I don't sound like *that* either."

"Yeah, you do," said Don. "Bertram and I make fun of you all the time. You're like a broken record. More like a puppet than a person. The other day Bertram almost had a heart attack when the chef told him you'd been down in the kitchen and you actually seemed to be enjoying something that wasn't … well, work or training or something."

Oh, that was the cherry on top of the ice cream I was going to have the chef teach me to make—cooking! I was actually good at cooking. Maybe I could cook for Odette, you know, to show her I was a normal person and not the Perfect Prince she thought I was. Yes, that was it.

I quickened my pace.

"There's no need to run away from me," said Don. "Anyway, take it up with Bertram. He started it."

"What?" The conversation we'd been having felt like a lifetime ago, even if only seconds had passed. "Oh, right. Yeah. No, I just really need that pen and paper. I don't want to forget this plan. It has to be perfect."

"You've got a really weird look on your face, James."

"It's called a smile, Don."

"I don't like it. It doesn't suit you."

I just laughed.

When we arrived at the bar I wasn't disappointed to reach it, although I certainly wouldn't be having any alcohol tonight. I tried to avoid Anita, too, because I'd just end up red-faced with embarrassment knowing how we knew each other, and I didn't want that kind of thing on my mind when I was planning something for Odette.

Odette was too ...

She was above it. She was too pure, too gentle, too kind as a person. I didn't want anything tainting that view of her, the one it took so long to create.

"Your Highness!" beamed Ritchie, slamming a hand down on the bar. "Oh, you're becoming a real regular. What can I get you?"

"A pen, or a quill, a pencil, or just a chunk of lead, and a piece of paper, my good man," I declared, "and one of those fizzy cream drinks. Cream soda? Whatever it's called. I've got some plans to make."

"Oh? Royal plans?" asked Ritchie with a chuckle, diving beneath the bar and pulling out a glass to get my drink first.

"Surprisingly, no," I said.

And for the first time in a long time, that didn't bother me. For the first time in longer than I could remember, all I cared about was making a thoroughly non-royal affair go well.

16
Odette

He acted like everything was normal. Just when I thought he was starting to listen, he didn't seem to realize he'd upset me yet again.

I didn't need him to give up going out and stay with me, but an invitation to go with him would've been nice. It wasn't really my scene, but I would've gone, just to stay with him.

Well, that was new. I'd always *somewhat* liked being around him, despite how *irritating* he was, but never had I *missed* it when I wasn't with him.

I was getting too close.

"What are you doing today?" asked James.

"Reading," I stated.

"Oh, great. Library again? I'll promise to be quiet and won't interrupt you."

"Actually, I was going to read in my room."

"Oh," said James. His face fell. "Oh … okay. Will you be out at all today? Last time you decided to read in your room I didn't see you again until almost midnight."

"No, I don't think I will," I said.

I could've offered him an explanation, told him what was so fascinating that I'd be spending the entire day studying it, pouring over pages without want for interaction with anybody else.

But then, last night I told him what was on my mind, and he'd left anyway, so what was the point? Either he wouldn't care, or he would care and it would just make the next time he chose Donald over me that much harder.

If he was always going to pick his best friend over me, I wasn't going to let myself get hurt. I didn't want a life where, just as we were starting to get along, he ran off to be with someone else.

It would hurt less if I kept my distance before the wedding. Then, when married, we could be allies. Maybe friends, but nothing more than the type of friends we were now.

Once in my room, I stared at the calendar, awaiting the day I turned 18 and could begin putting that distance between us. It would probably upset Queen Euberta, perhaps disappoint father, and even Bertram would surely be upset, too.

The next morning I shut myself in my room again, reading, and I managed to sneak out while the Prince was occupied . I spent most of my time in a little nook by the forest. When I came in I brushed James off and retired to bed.

One day to go. Another spent alone.

A night on a boat, then a day of being preened for the ball. Having your eyebrows plucked really did sting, and I disliked the extravagance of the dress they put me in. I needed to ask for a new beauty team. One who actually listened to my wishes. Putting in that request was the last thing I did before the ball began.

My last night with James for two years.

Father had gone all out. The music was upbeat and there was a singer joining the band. Guests knew not to be overly courteous to me, and only my favorite nobles were allowed in the main ballroom. Everybody else socialized up on the balconies or in the entrance hall.

I danced with all the people who looked after me when I was little when my parents were away on royal duties, had tea with Queen Euberta at one of the little tables in the corner, and had a spin with Bertram to one of the silliest songs that played all night.

Bright colors decorated the walls, the windows stood open to let in the night breeze and the sounds of nature, and father kept his speech short and didn't require me to give one at all.

He really had made this ball perfect for me.

"See, I told you you'd enjoy it," said father at the midway point, as we sat side-by-side on our thrones.

I only felt comfortable taking a break because James was engaged in conversation with somebody down by one of the windows. I skirted him all night, giving more of myself to guests than I pleased, laughing with people who I hadn't seen since I was a child, whose names I no longer remembered.

"I never doubted you for a second, father," I stated, grinning. "You're the only person I can trust to do right by me."

He leaned down and patted my hand. In two years I'd be upgraded to a throne as high as his, and one day I'd sit where my father sat. Well, I probably sit next to it actually, since that was throne was designed specifically for a king.

"Have you and Prince James had a fight, by the way?" asked father. "Because he says he hasn't spoken to you much tonight, or in recent days. And he'd like to. He says he'd like to do something to celebrate your birthday privately. He seemed enthused. And I'd take him up on his offer, because I've never heard anything like it from him. Who knows if he'll ever offer it again?" father chuckled.

I smiled wryly. "Yes. Who knows."

I supposed it was time. Pushing myself up like I was 80 and not 18, I made my way into the crowd which parted to allow me passage. Lord Marcum tapped James's shoulder and pointed at my approach, so I had him all to myself by the time I came to a stop.

"Odette," he said.

"I'm an adult now," I said flatly, "you have to call me Princess."

"Oh, please," James scoffed. "Right. It's not like you call me Prince. I think we've known each other too long for those kinds of formalities, don't you think?"

Formalities were exactly what we needed, since breaking down barriers would only lead to me getting hurt.

"It's Princess, Prince James," I stated. My eyes were focused, trained on him, trying to take in the entity that was the rigid Prince James in his royal attire and his dutiful pose. Not the person I started to see beneath that. "Anyway, I just came to thank you for coming. I know you're duty-bound to, but you didn't have to be on time, or stay the entire time, or mingle with other guests so nicely. In short, we appreciate your participation."

"'Appreciate your participation?'" said James. "That doesn't sound like you, Odette. It sounds … it sounds like the royal book of rules talking."

"It's Princess," I corrected him. "Princess, until the day we get married. Then, as allies, we can drop such formalities if you wish."

"Allies?"

I looked down. "Anyway, I should get back to my father. He worked hard on this ball, and he says they're serving turkey legs towards the end. They've always been my favorite, so, I should go mingle some more so it doesn't seem rude when I abandon everyone for them." I laughed, despite myself, but tried to keep the rest of my emotions in.

"Now, that sounds like the Odette I know," said James.

"It's Princess," I repeated.

I gave him one last look, a sweeping glance from head to toe. I took in the unchanging boy into man who always dressed in the same stiff attire with the same annoyingly perfect haircut curling under his chin. Hair plastered with too much gel to keep the curls down. Curls I'd seen just once, one summer when Donald pushed him into a lake during a walk and his hair dried in the sun.

I rejoined my father on the throne. Next time he asked about James, I'd change the subject to express my gratitude about the ball again, particularly about the chocolate fountain that made its appearance alongside the turkey legs, and these strange fizzy fruity alcoholic drinks father thought I would like.

The drinks Donald took James out for several nights earlier. Drinks I would have discovered and liked had he just asked me to come.

Yet my father knew me well enough to know I'd like these even though I'd never tried them. It was clear he was the only person in my life who truly cared. I had to hold onto that.

Once the music finally died and everything was cleared away, I felt like I could breathe for the first time all night. Father seemed to expect that I would open up to him once I changed out of my heavy dress and wiped off the make up that felt slick on my face, but I just told him I was going to bed.

Before I went, I gave Queen Euberta a gracious thanks for coming, and asked Bertram where he'd be in half an hour. It would be an hour before the royal boat could dock, as some of the nobles who lived away now had to take boats to get home to their towns.

Once I knew everything would go to plan, I went to my room and penned a letter.

It wasn't the first time I'd written to James. I'd left him plenty of little notes over the years, obligatory notes thanking him for things, notes calling him out on his ridiculous ways, and of course, my detailed instructions when I was 13 on how he should rearrange his game room.

This one was as frank as all of them, perhaps even more curt.

"Princess," said Bertram sadly, when I met him in the library, "it's a real shame that you will be leaving us. Won't you at least come and tell him in person?"

I shook my head. "No. I'd rather not see Prince James, thank you, but I'll tell Queen Euberta. Where is she?"

"Having one last cup of tea with your father. I think it's a good thing she's with him, because if you tell them both at once, it's less stress on you tomorrow. I'll give this letter to James. And you know, I really thought you were starting to be friends. He had such plans for you, really, for a day he swears you'll enjoy."

I scoffed. "How would he know?"

Bertram sighed.

It was so odd. I'd seen his face almost every day of summer for years, and he'd always been unchanging, a staple popping up here and there who I didn't appreciate as much because I was always battling James and his silly best friend. Yet I felt like I was letting Bertram down, and saying goodbye to an old friend I'd barely gotten to know.

I'd certainly be letting Queen Euberta down, as I thought of our little evening teas and all those chats we had and how she treated me like I was her own.

And then there was James. He'd probably be disappointed. Apparently he *was* actually making an effort, but an effort made for something that was always going to be second to him wasn't the kind of effort I was interested in being made for me.

But yes, he would be disappointed.

"Do you think I'm making a mistake?" I asked.

Bertram put his hand on my shoulder.

"If this is what feels best, then it's impossible to make a mistake." He smiled, which he so rarely did genuinely. "The castle won't be the same without you, Princess. I don't know how I'll fill my summers now. It is always nice to have company during my breaks, and nicer still to know there were two young people livening up that old castle that had long since felt stale. But I suppose two years will pass ..." He clicked his fingers. "I know the last 11 have."

I gave him a genuine smile, too.

17

James

The paper almost crumpled in my hand, but I couldn't destroy the last letter she sent to me.

I knew I ruined it. The second I walked off with him, I knew. I just didn't expect the reaction to be this extreme.

"Come on, Bertram," I pleaded, "she must have said something. Anything more about why she's ending the visits."

"All I know is what's in the letter," said Bertram curtly.

"'Upon further evaluation of our relationship I think we suit each other better as allies rather than friends or potential romantic partners,'" I read. "Not even friends. And I thought … I had all these … these plans," I choked. "I was going to take her to a museum, and the place full of animals, then maybe make arrangements for next summer to take her to my aunt's house with the two huge libraries and the man who makes those weapons that you put a little bullet in and shoot. And I was going to cook for her, and … Well, I didn't know what was going to happen next, but I really wanted to find out. Do you think I should—"

Bertram raised a hand. "I think the situation is best left alone, James. Because she seemed upset enough when she handed me the letter. I can't imagine how she'd feel if she got one in return."

"But—"

"Odette has a past that's outside of you, James," said Bertram. "She never spoke of it specifically, but she alluded to it enough times to make me realize that even the smallest bit of direct rejection would one day be too much for her to take, so she distanced herself to avoid hurting herself further."

Rejection? I didn't. I never. But to her … maybe that was what it looked like when I went off with Don and left her behind.

"I don't know what you did to her, James, and I'm sure you didn't mean it, but it drove her away because she thought she'd get hurt again if she stayed. You might want to think about that so, I don't know, in two years you might begin repairing your relationship. Show her that not everyone in the world is going to choose somebody else over her."

It was like he'd thrown a boulder at my chest, then it turned into ice and wrapped itself around my heart. My throat felt funny, too.

Why did this bother me so much? I spent years trying to keep her at a distance, distance she was now requesting. I should've been okay with it, and maybe a few years ago I would've been thrilled—but then again at the end of the summer I'd always asked if she'd be coming the next year, and when mother confirmed she would be, I smiled.

"I didn't mean to do anything against her," I said. "Honestly, Bertram. I didn't."

Bertram smiled, but it didn't look real.

"I know," said Bertram, and he patted me on the shoulder and turned away.

With my castle feeling strangely empty, I turned to my desk to place the letter in with all the rest.

18

Stefan

"You know, Your Majesty, in my experience it's very unusual for a chef to be shown the ropes by the king."

The king raised his eyebrows, and in that moment I realized I'd said something just slightly off.

"In your experience? You said you've only ever cooked at home. How much experience can you have at 18?" the king chuckled.

"Well, in mean in my experience talking to other chefs and reading about these things. You know, I was meticulous when I was researching the job. Night chef in a castle ... not just an unusual position, but a highly intimidating one."

The king chuckled again and patted me on the shoulder. "Indeed it is. But I've always been happy to give jobs to people who need and deserve them. You traveled a long way, Stefan. How long is the voyage from your land to ours?"

"Three weeks by boat, Your Majesty, and it's not a fun one. I was deep in the belly of a wooden ship, stuck on a little bunk for most of it with my brother on the one below. People got sick rampantly, and not just seasick, but other kinds because we were all so pressed up against each other. My brother and I were the only ones who didn't seem to sleep. Awake all day as well as all night, because everybody was so noisy ..."

The look of sympathy on the king's face made knots form in my stomach, but I needed this. It was just money to send home to the kingdom so I felt like I was contributing, and being live-in gave me a place to spend my nights.

The hard part was over. I'd landed the job of night chef, baking for the next day and making sure the castle was well-stocked if anyone were to get up at night for something to eat—I just had to prove I could do it.

Luckily I spent most of my time in the kitchens growing up, so it wouldn't be too hard a task.

"Well, you'll never have an ordeal like that again if I've got anything to say about it," said the king. "Every morning just before the dawn you can report to Chef Julian, and if you ever have an issue he can't deal with, you ask for me. I treat my staff like family here. I don't believe in being all high and mighty. There's no need to call me Your Majesty, either, just King Richard will do. And even the king part it took me a long time to grow to like. I look forward to seeing what you can produce for us, Stefan."

"As do I, King Richard."

He left me to a kitchen smaller then the one I grew up using, but then again, the entire castle was smaller than any other I'd been in.

But despite its size, I had no objections to its layout or construction. Sturdy stone walls, all the latest appliances, connected to a little roomful of wood to fire the ovens up.

As I ran my fingers over the wood for the second time—the first being during my demonstration to show I was good enough for this job—I appreciated its fine quality once again.

It wasn't that splinty stuff covered in bark. These were well chopped logs and smooth enough to run a finger over, good enough to stock a king's fireplace in his chambers. Well, or at least a prince's, in my experience.

I walked up and down the kitchen, eager to get started, but mostly I just wanted to relax. I hadn't endured quite the journey I described—although it was equally poor, spending my days hiding and trying not to get stepped on and spending my nights hiding in trying not to get caught as a stowaway—but I was ready for relaxation.

I could be safe here. He wasn't going to come back and try to attack. He couldn't get through the guards. He said it himself when he came home to try and take what was to be my brother's.

I sat on one of the high stools which I definitely appreciated. So few kitchens—and I'd seen quite a few when I was young, just developing a passion for cooking as I visited Lords' houses and big restaurants around my land—provided seating for the workers who'd be chopping and mixing and doing all of these things all day long.

My legs usually ached after a hard day of baking, standing in one spot. By the end of it I was desperate to wake my muscles which were stuck in a statuesque standing pose. I bounced more than a frog would to waken myself up.

And I'd know.

So you like it, then?

I smiled. I'd really need to learn to hide my thoughts, but these were ones I didn't mind sharing so much. The only upside to this curse was having someone in it with me, making sure I wasn't alone no matter what I was doing or worse.

"Yes, I like it. How is your stable?"

It's big and cozy, and the horses aren't as high maintenance as he said they'd be. I could hear the smile in his internal voice. *I really like this king. Even our own father thought it was insane to let someone stay with the horses all night. But I wouldn't leave them alone. They're just big babies really. Big, cuddly babies. They're like giant dogs who you can ride around on and who make loud noises.*

I laughed. "You say that about every animal. You said it about cows. You said it about sheep. I can kind of see it with cows, especially the one who used to hug you, but sheep and horses? No."

Well, whatever, said Gabriel. *I'm just saying, I love the king. I love these horses. I love my life. I'd rather be at home in my featherbed, but you know, this isn't too bad.*

"I love the king too," I said. "He is very nice. Very genuine. More humble than I've heard the kings in this land are usually. But you can't give him all the credit—the king said his daughter is the one who wants the horses tended to by night. The king's daughter sounds nice."

"Oh, does she?"

I almost fell off my chair.

"Did I say that out loud?"

I'm talking out loud too, said Gabriel. *The horses think I'm insane. Some seem to enjoy it. I'm still not used to doing it all in my head when I actually have a voice. I'll work on it.*

I bit my tongue. *Me too.*

"Em, Hello. Sorry. You might think I'm crazy talking to myself out loud, but I was just ... speaking to the kitchen."

There was a girl about my age in the doorway. Maybe a little bit younger? No more than 18 surely, and a beauty.

She had this mane of silvery white hair tied back, a stunning face with this kind of subtle cuteness mixed with a more intense kind of beauty.

She had a long and slender neck and stood before me with a slight slouch to her shoulders. She wore a light cotton shirt tucked into a long kind of skirt/pantaloons thing that looked like it was both at the same time. The kind of casual clothing often worn by schoolteachers where I was from, who wanted the convenience of trousers but the chic appearance of a skirt.

"I talk to myself out loud, too," said the girl. "Don't worry. Well, I do it less nowadays because people tend to listen in and hear me, but I did it all the time when I was young. It used to bother people then, actually. But it doesn't bother me. Sorry for interrupting your conversation."

I let out a laugh that came out far too high pitched in a little bit shrieky.

"My conversation is done, miss," I said.

"So why is the princess nice?"

I smiled. "She likes horses. My brother is the new night stable manager. It's his job to sleep with the horses and keep them company. I know, it might sound insane, but trust me, it's very beneficial. Animals feel closer to you and trust you more if they have kind of an intimate relationship with you. Like a dog who shares your bed will be your companion for life and trust you no matter what you do."

"Well, horses are just big dogs you can ride around on," said the girl, and it gave me pause. "I asked my father if I could sleep with them numerous times, but apparently it's not becoming of a princess." She strode towards me and put out her hand. "Odette," she said.

"Princess Odette," I repeated, in awe.

She looked nothing like a princess. Well, she was pretty like one, but she was so ... normal. Her clothes, the way she stood. I'd never seen a princess like this, because they were also obsessed with keeping up appearances when they were around me.

Then again, they usually wanted to marry me, but I did not want them in return. I was more interested in a close relationship that didn't involve legally binding yourself to someone. It made it feel more natural, you know? Like it was a choice rather than a necessity.

"I'm Stefan," I said.

"The new night chef?"

"Yes, Princess Odette."

"Oh, please. There's no need to call me Princess." She moved into the room and hopped up on a stool across from me. A Princess sitting across from a chef. So unusual, and yet from someone who asked to sleep with horses, I didn't find it all that strange.

"I was just getting used to the environment before beginning work," I said quickly.

"Oh no, I assumed as much. I just came down to say hello. You see, I'll probably be bothering you a lot as time goes on. I get up a lot at night. Like clockwork, every night around midnight, I'm awake and wandering the castle. I used to love talking to our old night chef. He'd tell me stories about his grandchildren and let me 'help' him bake. By that I mean he let me lick the spoons because I'm terrible and anything I make is likely to blow up."

A chuckle. "Oh, Princess, I hardly find that believable. Oh, sorry, I mean, Odette."

"Well, trust me. If you ever let me near your baking equipment, you'll see."

My heart pounded much too quickly in my chest. There was no need for this. She was just a person, like me, *very* like me ... only she didn't know it.

"So you're also nocturnal?" I asked.

"Oh, yes. I go to bed late, and a couple of hours later I'm up. Twenty minutes to an hour of walking around and talking later, I'll being sleep again and up around dawn. Hence I requested to sleep with the horses, especially now that I no longer travel away during summers so I can stay with them every night, but ..." She flapped a hand. "Doesn't matter."

I immediately needed to know everything. I wanted to know why she was away during the summers, and why it made her look at the ground and form creases around her eyes, like it was something she regretted. But I would say nothing. I was staff, and no princess would want to have anything to do with a lowly chef.

"Anyway, I should go," said the princess, "I have a couple of things I want to get done before bed. Re-organizing my to-be-read list and whatnot. I might see you around midnight most nights, but there's no promise. It was good to meet you, Stefan."

"You too, Odette," I said, and I very almost gave her a bow as she left, but I just about managed to keep upright. Something told me she wouldn't like that kind of formality.

And so I began my duties. Little pastries and cakes and muffins and all these things, enough to feed the entire staff, far more grand than most kings would feed their staff with.

I took my time and swore I wouldn't stop until midnight, but an hour passed and there was no sign of the princess.

I deemed it safe to take a small nap in the log room, because I just couldn't sleep deeply during the day. Once I woke I put the finishing touches on some of the treats I was leaving to cool, and my first work night was done.

I left the castle through the servant's entrance, although the king didn't like to call it that. I hurried into the forest to the work to await the rising sun. The king would think I was in my room.

And now I would wait out the day, hopefully sleep, find some refreshment in that cute little pond I scoped out on the grounds, and wait for the night once more.

I dozed on a lily pad for a couple of hours, but it was nothing compared to the sleep I had as a human. I was joined by my brother shortly after, croaking away on another pad. Eventually he settled down to sleep too.

We didn't talk much by day, although I did see some of his dreams. He wasn't yet good at blocking out his thoughts.

My mind wandered, trying to occupy itself so I wouldn't invade his privacy. I tried to focus on important things.

For example, *him*. He was connected to us, too. Part of what he called a "pack", technically. But because he was the leader, were his thoughts protected, or was he just so good at keeping them to himself that he was silent and listening, but not giving us anything to listen to?

Time would tell, I supposed. Or maybe it wouldn't.

Maybe sleeping was the only way to block out my brother, and in sleep I wouldn't be thinking of *him*.

He was around here somewhere, he'd said it: "I'll return to where I last came from, then. To my last hope. And this time I'll succeed."

He would not succeed, but he would still wait in hope that he could make another move. I knew it.

And he was definitely here, because we had to go where he went. It was like a draw, something that pulled us to him. Why else would we have chosen such a small town in the smallest kingdom in this landmass? It would be far easier to blend in somewhere larger.

More unpleasant thoughts. Yes, sleeping wa—

"Oh, hello!"

My eyes snapped open and I let out a loud involuntary croak. I knew that voice.

Princess! I tried to say, but it was just another croak.

"Look at you two! Oh, you're adorable. I've been watching you for a few days. Are you all settled in? I hope so. The last frog I met out here hopped away and never came back. And now there are two of you! Oh, aren't you cute? I love your eyes."

If I looked down, would that be to much not like a frog? I knew our eyes weren't that of typical amphibians, but it wasn't noticeable from a distance.

Our eyes were too human, something *he* warned us about. All while apologizing for lashing out, but saying it was the "only way to keep everybody in our kingdom safe." Oh yes, turning the princes into frogs was the only way to keep the kingdom safe. Great logic.

"I'm Odette," said the princess. "Don't worry, I'm a friend. I like animals. I like talking to them. And watching. Studying, really. I know it sounds insane. There's only one person I ever told that who didn't call me insane for it, or laugh at me for it—that was Prince James, but we don't like him. Okay? We don't like Prince James, because if we like him, we'll just get all sad when he likes other people more than us." She winced. "And we have to marry him in two years. Well, I do. You don't. Frogs are lucky like that."

Princess Odette giggled, and I was captivated. This made up for her not showing up last night.

Gabriel was thoroughly awake now, laughing at me in his head, but I didn't care. Princess Odette could talk to me forever and I'd be okay with it.

"Here's the deal," said the princess. "We like the king, we like Lord Tyrone, I'll complain to you a lot about Lady Essi and Lord Benni and the new silk seller in town, I'll definitely complain to you about having to headline The Festival of Crows, and I'll probably read to you quite a lot, but you'll probably be really bored by the kind of books I read."

If I had paper and opposable thumbs I'd write down every word.

"Oh, and I almost forgot, we like Stefan, the new night chef. And I guess Ella, the baker from the village, too. She always gives me rolls for parents with young children. She did that the other day when I ventured out into the village for the first time in a while. It was good fun, actually."

Yeah? Why was it fun? I asked, but it came as another croak.

"I try not to go out there a lot," said Odette. "And I only ever stay until before it gets dark. The last time I was there after dark ..." She shut her eyes and shook her head. "But it's nice during the day, especially if you stay out of all the little alleyways. It's safe when you're surrounded by people and light. Even if those people are a little ... strange sometimes," she laughed.

How strange, Odette?

"For example, the other day I met a strange man in a cloak. It wasn't the typical cloak worn by people who come from other towns in our kingdom, so I knew he must be very far from home. I asked him if he needed help, but he looked like I'd just asking if he wanted to be murdered or something. He started panicking, so I wondered if it would comfort him if I showed him my face instead of being a creepy cloaked stranger. That seemed to terrify him even more. He ran away apologizing. He seemed nice, but easily spooked. I liked his hair. It was red. I don't usually see a lot of people with red hair around here, do you?"

A redhaired man in a cloak who ran away? My stomach lurched and I felt I could vomit up everything I'd eaten as a human last night even though this was a completely different body.

There was only one person that could be, and if he saw Odette's face, then ...

But no. He hadn't acted. And hopefully, he wouldn't.

Funny he ran away, said Gabriel, but I just shrugged. Well, I would have if I could.

Probably wasn't ready to attack yet, I said.

Too many witnesses, said Gabriel.

Yes, let's hope it stays that way. I should suggest to the king to employ more guards. Pretend I saw some figures lurking ...

"So, while out in the village, you'll never guess what I bought," said Odette, and I tried to keep listening but my mind kept wandering.

Matteo. How could I stop Matteo? By day there was nothing I could do, and by night, the guards. I had to get *all the guards*. And keep a lookout.

He *couldn't* attack, unless his powers grew. And there was no way of knowing if they'd grow.

If he did attack, he'd said his plan was to attack the king. Not her. He never mentioned *her*.

I hoped he hadn't mentioned Odette because he wouldn't *hurt* Odette, but it didn't seem very likely, did it?

But as long as I was here, I would do everything in my power to defend her and keep them at bay.

19

Matteo

This was my last chance to get this right.

I knew I shouldn't have gone home, but I thought maybe if I tried to explain ...

But they didn't listen. Why would they? The bastard brother who tormented them had returned to do the same thing all over again. *I* wouldn't listen. And now they were damned, trapped, and everyone was going to die.

It probably wasn't the best night to be doing this. But on the other hand, it *was* the best night, because everybody would be so merry that they wouldn't notice an extra animal in the woods or little fly buzzing around the corridors.

There were plenty of windows open due to the nice summer weather, so I could go in and out as I pleased, scoping the place out. It was safe for me to spend the day inside, as long as there were no spiders around, but it seemed like attacking from outside was the better idea.

Bursting through a window or ... oh but then, that would weaken me. Perhaps I ought to wait for the princess to go off alone instead.

She was alone now, but it was too early. She wasn't officially of age until the ball, so my plan wouldn't be all that effective. Even if she agreed to do what I asked, it would hold no weight. And her father most certainly wouldn't throw a ball for her after making that agreement.

"Father says it won't be that bad," she told a frog. No, hold on. That was Gabriel. If flies could laugh ..."Although, he did say he had 'a little extra padding' on his chest and back, so it will probably be a lot more painful on my legs where there's none, especially the ankles and knees."

The princess shuddered, and I with her. "Beautification" was barbaric. Then again, what I was planning was worse.

"I've had the eyebrows off, so that'll be fine. I'm not really looking forward to having my hair straightened, because I don't know how long it will get, and long hair is harder to look after. Mother always had help doing hers. I don't know how Queen Euberta does it. She must have a team of 10 working on her every single morning to get it up way she has it. Oh, remember I told you about her? I can't wait to see her again. I've missed her. First thing tomorrow I'm going to invite her to tea. She always threw such good little evening tea sessions for me, so tomorrow night, I want to do the same for her."

Queen Euberta. I remembered watching her. She seemed nice, if not slightly annoying. Everyone was so ... *nice*. Especially the princess. How could I look at her here, knowing what I had to do? I still saw that innocent little girl from the first attack.

And Queen Euberta would certainly be a fierce protector of her, more fierce than she knew.

I landed on a nearby bush, but a spider lurked close so I flew off again and landed on the bench behind Odette instead. Another little frog hopped forward. This one eyed me up. Oh, how ironic would it be for Stefan to eat me? I had to go flying again. Maybe change into a wolf in the woods. Wolves had excellent hearing, didn't they?

It would be difficult to keep safe. More difficult than I thought. Especially since the ballroom was right next to the garden, full of actual bugs. And someone would definitely notice a fly staying oddly still just outside the window.

"Marnin'," said a voice I didn't recognize, just after I transformed. "I've been sent to get you, Princess. It's time to start. The whole beauty team is up there waiting."

"Oh, wonderful," muttered Odette. "And you're ..." She paused. "Jaunty. I remember. Well, you're certainly acting it. Is the rest of my new beauty team as seemingly approachable as you are? Because my last one was stern and didn't listen to a thing I said."

"Believe me, Princess, your father hand-picked us all. Plain dress, subtle make up. Boring for my taste. I think you'd look good with a mullet and some kind of extreme attire. But what do I know, hey? Let's go."

Their footsteps and voices grew further and further away. Odette would be away with her beauty team *all* day, so I had neither need nor want to spy on her.

She'd already have enough people invading her privacy. Poor Princess. That was the one thing that really grateful I'd never have to inherit.

When I was king of her kingdom, I would definitely abolish the rules that princesses had to be plucked and preened and scrubbed to be made "presentable" when they came of age.

But that was all something to worry about in the future. Not now.

I had to get out of the woods. Who knew who would venture in here and find it odd to see a wolf just lying there, creepily still, with eerily human eyes? Anyone who knew anything about the mysterious would be able to identify me as more than a wolf in an instant.

So it was back to being a fly, this time on a brightly lit wall in the castle. No spiders to be seen. Just people running up and down decorating everywhere guests might walk, followed by the loud arrival of the queen who foiled me last time.

"Queen Euberta. Prince James. It's been far too long. Oh, I've missed being around you." The King sounded sincere.

"Oh, it has, my dear King Richard, it really has."

"Your Majesty," said a young man at her side. The young man Odette was to marry. She was lucky. He was the kind of handsome that I, even in my natural form, wasn't. The kind of handsome a prince should be. And such great hair.

"Prince James," said King Richard. "I'm so pleased you're here. And I'm sure after some time apart Princess Odette will be dying to see you and get to know you as the man you've grown into. My my, you look so grown-up. So handsome. You're putting me to shame as the most handsome man in the kingdom."

James laughed cordially, and the king gave him a wink. Gods, these people were so nice. Why did they have to be so damn nice?

"Where is Princess Odette?" asked James. "I'd like to see her. It's been too long. And I don't think we left things very ... well, she called off our summer visits, so I think that sentence speaks for itself."

"Away with her beauty team, I'm afraid," said King Richard, "but I'm sure she'll be done an hour or two before the ball, so perhaps you can catch up with her then. She'll likely be in the library."

"She hasn't changed much, then, has she?"

"Oh no, she's still the same Princess Odette you knew and ... well, I'm not going to say loved, but you get the idea."

"So there's no chance I could go and speak to her now?"

"James," the queen scolded. "A Princess must not be disturbed during her Coming-of-Age preparations. Only her parents are allowed to stop in. Oh, she's going to look so pretty. I can't wait to see her again. I've asked Bertram to bring my tea set. I'd love to arrange one of our little evening tea sessions like we used to have. Tomorrow night, of course, and then, if you're both still keen, we'll begin preparations for the wedding!"

James smiled stiffly. Even though it was tiny and I had no idea where it was located, I felt like my heart was squeezing itself much too hard for my liking.

Oh, if only I didn't have to do this. If only they could have that tea. But the lives of many were more important than the hearts and wishes of two.

"Come on," said the king, "let me show you to your rooms personally. Oh, and you'll have to meet some of our new staff. Especially our night chef, Stefan. Though he's never around during the day. Perhaps he'll be at the ball. I did invite him. I'm not sure if he'll go. He's very quiet and likes to keep to himself. Oh, and James, you must tell me about your training. I hear you entered into some royal archery competitions between various kingdoms ..."

I tuned out their chatter as they moved off. I considered following, but what would be the point? This seemed as good a place as any to spend the rest of my day, my blood boiling in my tiny fly body, my head reeling.

It was very hard to tune out my own thoughts, and harder still to tune out the other chatter going on in the back of my mind. But I had to do it.

I had to do everything I had planned today, otherwise innocent people would die. And it was better innocent people suffered and bent to new rules rather than let another group die because a kingdom couldn't reform.

Read on for a free chapter of the first book in this trilogy, *The Swan's Prince*.

Do you want a further four chapters for free? Click here[1] or go to my author page on Amazon to sign up for my newsletter.

---

1.   https://mailchi.mp/277ae6788298/ellia-embers-newsletter

1

Odette

"I know this is arduous, Odette, but we all went through it. You're of age now, and being of age means you have to look and present yourself a certain way."

My father, the noble King Richard of Swanwood, stroked my hair gently, and I winced as my flesh was torn from the bone and blood poured into the bathwater.

Okay, I was being dramatic. I was having the hair *ripped* out of my legs. At that moment, I wished I were a bird so I could molt and my old feathers would just fall away.

Or I wished I was a prince and not a princess. Princes didn't have their legs waxed.

Or maybe I just wished royal women didn't have to be plucked like a goose the minute they turned 20.

"Oh. So *you* had to have your body torn apart when you were my age, did you?"

My father chuckled, patted the air next to my head, then patted my head as he felt it out. He couldn't see me—his gaze was set determinedly away, because having him watching me waxed in the bath would be pretty strange.

"Not my legs, no. But my chest, my back ..." He shuddered, the hand vibrating in my untameable hair. "For the first time in my life, I wished to be a commoner that day. You see it when they remove their shirts to work in the summer sun. Hair from shoulders to hips, and nobody ridicules them for it. But it's not becoming of a royal."

My father paused. It wouldn't have surprised me if he'd forgotten why he'd come in. He'd delivered news and gotten distracted, as usual, but it made me smile.

"Anyway," he said, sighing, "I'll give you your privacy for the rest of this … um, milestone."

Milestone … I knew my father well enough to know he was going to call it what it was: an ordeal.

And all for a man I didn't like, for a kingdom I was going to inherit no matter what.

"The pain doesn't last, princess," said River, one of the only nice people on my team today. "It's harsh, but you get used to it, and the water has eucalyptus in it. And we're getting the worst part out of the way first."

"Well, thank goodness for that."

Her smile was sad, and I almost felt bad about my sarcasm.

So I sat there in the cooling water with bubbles from my knees to my neck, letting them preen me. Apparently I had "startlingly hairy toes" and "a stubborn little patch there" behind my knees. But River was right. The water soothed my burning skin and I relaxed to enjoy my bath …

… for 30 seconds, and then they moved on to my arms and hands.

Then, finally, with all four limbs and a patch of my abdomen stinging, they left me to enjoy my bath for a whole 20 minutes. Wonderful.

"Don't worry, princess," said River, attempting what had to be a comforting smile as she and the rest of the beauty team left, "I promise it does get easier, and this is nothing compared to what we'll have to do before your wedding night."

I shuddered as she closed the door behind her.

I didn't blame my beauty team. They were just doing their jobs. It was customary for a princess to be plucked and pruned and made over entirely. We had to look the part of, well, princess. I'd been *lucky* my whole life. I spent my childhood and teen years in dirty pants full of holes and covered in stains. I wore my bushy hair in a huge bun or a pair of braids, never caring for it.

No wonder Prince James hated me after our first summer together. I was a mess and a menace.

We started spending July until September together when I was seven, almost eight, and we never got along. The princesses of *his* kingdom were forced to be prim and proper and perfect their whole lives. The poor girls never got to be kids. I must've been a beast compared to his elegant cousins who visited on holidays and other occasions.

He'd admitted as much towards the end of our visits, when were starting to get along. Only to ruin our budding friendship by doing something to hurt me.

Luckily I hadn't seen him in two years. As soon as I got autonomy at 18, I put an end to those summer visits. It was better to stop seeing him than to risk getting hurt for another two years. I knew I'd still have to marry him, but it didn't mean I had to see him a moment more than I needed to.

"You can still back out, you know," my father told me as my team combed their way through my wet rattail curls once they peeled me and my sensitive skin out of the tub. "Queen Euberta and I have encouraged this your whole lives, but we've never *forced* the marriage upon you. What I want most is for you to be happy."

"And I want *you* to be happy, father." I moved, and my team stopped brushing immediately. I faced my father, whose facial lines had only deepened with age, and today they deepened further with worry. "And you won't be happy if you're constantly worried about money. We need to merge with a wealthy kingdom or we may not be able to sustain our lands for another royal generation. And I'm the key to that."

He looked 10 years younger when he smiled, but his eyes still held such sadness for me. Gods, I loved my father.

"I can still marry Queen Euberta instead, you know. Yes, that would mean Prince James would be king due to his being older than you, but I'm sure you two could come to some sort of agreement to rule as equals after mine and Queen Euberta's deaths."

I winced automatically. My mother's death left a hole in my heart that could never be mended. I didn't need to think about my father's too.

"You swore you'd never marry after mother died." I swallowed back the tears that threatened to form. "And I want to honor that wish. I'll marry Prince James. I'll complain all the time and you'll owe me for the rest of your life, but I'm in if he is."

"And he very much is. He knows how much his mother enjoys her solitude now that his father is gone."

Queen Euberta's husband had been dead since James was young, and she'd flourished in that time. She'd married the king before she was of age, as her family had money and the royals desperately needed it. She'd never been an adult alone. *Now* was her time to thrive.

I'd had two years of adulthood freedom alone, in my youth and everything, and she never had that. I didn't want to lose this, but I wanted my father happy more. I could find a way to make this thing with Prince James work, as much as I was dreading his appearance at my Coming-of-Age ball.

I last saw him at the ball for my 18th, and that hadn't been our finest meeting.

My father patted my hair and left me in the careful hands of my beauty team. I had nobody to tell me if what they were doing to my hair was working, or even if I'd look like myself at all once they were done with me. But little my little, more hair dropped to hang around my shoulders.

"We have a special salve, for it," said River, when she noticed me looking. "Tames the hair and keeps it neat. All the prettiest royals use it."

I wished I had someone to talk to about how little I cared about being pretty.

They let me inspect myself in the mirror once they'd finished with me, and I hardly knew myself. My hair was all straight and shiny. It was still thick, but it was tamable. It looked less like a white bush around my head, and instead I looked like the pretty women I saw making their way around the castle with their pale blonde locks thoroughly in check.

"Elegant," River told me. "Very elegant. Like a dove. Or like something fiercer. A swan, maybe."

I mustered up a laugh there was no real weight behind.

"I still think she'd look better with a mullet," said Jaunty. "Everyone in the northern kingdoms is wearing them."

River grinned at him, shook her head, and he said nothing more.

"And now, your dress," said Katie. "I was thinking of something in magenta."

"Magenta is too vivid," said a member of my team who'd yet to speak today. "She needs something soft and light. She's coming of age, not announcing her availability to all the young princes after being widowed in her 20s. She needs something as light and pretty as she is. Something like ..."

The unnamed person scurried away, and when he returned, he was holding a very simple pink dress that I knew would be form-fitting and comfortable.

This sparked and argument about it being *too* simple, but I put my foot down for the first time all day.

"It's perfect," I declared; it reminded me of one of the last my mother bought me. "It's the one I'll wear to the ball. Thank you all for your help, and you can go now."

"Go?" laughed Petruchio. "No, no. Now it's time for makeup. And as George said, we need it to be soft and light. Something perfect for the heir to the throne Coming-of-Age."

I sighed, and so began yet another ordeal.

This time I ignored the arguments and smaller disagreements about what my makeup ought to be like. I just shut my eyes and let them get on with it, and I didn't care to examine myself in the mirror again once it was done. I was always told I had such a pretty face, and I should treat it well. So why they wanted to cover it up with paint that felt heavy on my skin was beyond me.

"And now you're perfect for the ball," said Alexa. I wished they'd just let one of the team do the talking, because it was getting hard to keep track of names and faces. I was cheering myself on just for remembering so many after they introduced themselves to me this morning.

Then I realized the one who'd just spoken was called Tanner, and my cheering died as quickly as it was birthed.

Once I was ready, I still had an hour to go before the ball. I hardly knew what to do with myself as servants ran around the castle, calling instructions and reminders to each other.

I sought solitude, and the only place I knew nobody would be running was the library. So I dashed off there, dressed in my ballgown with my hair and makeup done, not caring who saw me.

And when I say I ran, I *ran*. I didn't want compliments from anyone, and I didn't want anyone to bother me or tell me I shouldn't be out of my room before the ball.

Nobody spoke to me. When the princess ran around the castle, they knew she meant business. I didn't even *expect* anyone to bat an eyelid, and definitely not call out, but then—

"Hey! Excuse me! Does anyone know where the library is?"

The man's voice was familiar, half drowned out by my footsteps, and he probably wasn't talking to me, but I called, "Follow me. I'm heading there now."

A set of footsteps joined mine. Whoever it was seemed to be staying far enough behind me to not trod on my dress. He asked, "Excuse me, but why are we running?"

"To get there faster!"

"Sounds like a plan to me!"

The oak double doors of the library swam into view, and I didn't stop when I reached them. I pounded right through, and whoever was behind me did too. I stopped just before the first set of bookshelves.

And he didn't.

I tumbled *into* the set of bookshelves, and the man fell on top of me with a gasp. The books clattered us over the head, probably bruising the arms I raised to protect myself as he climbed off and I got to my feet.

It wasn't my first time breaking a man's fall. Prince James landed on me when his treehouse collapsed when I was 13. At least this time I didn't break anything.

"I'm sorry! I'm so sorry, I didn't mean—you stopped so—Princess Odette?"

When he said my name, I knew why his voice was familiar. And then his face was familiar, but it was kinder than I'd ever seen it. His eyes were full of concern, set into a face more handsome than I remembered since I'd last seen it two years ago.

My heart started pounding. I wasn't supposed to be pleased to see him. I wasn't supposed to feel all those *things* I started feeling the night we truly connected for the first time. The night he listened to me about things nobody else did, and didn't tease me for all I said.

The night I realized that no matter how nice he was to me after all our years of knowing each other, he could still hurt me.

There was something different about him. Perhaps it was his hairstyle that struck me, made him more appealing. He'd had his hair in this weird kind of bob with full bangs, but now he'd let it grow longer, thicker, fuller, in curls down his shoulders with bangs that swooped over to one side.

He was the prettiest man I'd ever seen.

It was too bad I knew him well enough to know his insides didn't match.